THE THIRTEENTH ROOM

ADAM CROFT

GET MORE OF MY BOOKS FREE!

To say thank you for buying this book, I'd like to invite you to my exclusive *VIP Club*, and give you some of my books and short stories for FREE.

To join the club, head to adamcroft.net/vip-club and two free books will be sent to you straight away! And the best thing is it won't cost you a penny — ever.

Adam Croft

For more information, visit my website: adamcroft.net

BOOKS IN THIS SERIES

Books in the Kempston Hardwick series so far:
1. Exit Stage Left
2. The Westerlea House Mystery
3. Death Under the Sun
4. The Thirteenth Room

To find out more about this series and others, please head to adamcroft.net/list.

THURSDAY 12TH MARCH

Elliot Carr closed his eyes and turned his head upwards as he tried to blot out the inevitable argument which had ensued. They could never go anywhere — anywhere — without some sort of drama from Scarlett.

He'd known she was a drama queen when he'd first met her, but that was one of things that had first attracted him to her. It was certainly far less irritating than that erroneous extra 't' at the end of her name, which her parents had added in order to make her name 'unique' and 'different'. Everything her parents had ever done had been unique and different, so why would they stop at naming their child?

If the truth be told, it was Scarlett's parents he disliked. Sure, Scarlett had her pretensions, her airs and graces, but she couldn't be blamed for them. It was purely down to her parents, who'd led her to believe that she had some sort of divine right over other people just because her father was a banker and her mother had delusions of being a successful novelist. Elliot had always tried to stifle the laughter when Irma told people she was a full-time writer. Sure, she spent all of her time writing, but she'd never earned a penny from it. That didn't bother her. She didn't need to, what with Robert raking home in a week what most people could only hope to earn in a year.

Where Elliot came from, money didn't make someone a better person. In fact, he found that the opposite was usually true. His more modest upbringing though, had brought with it a certain talent for tact and tongue-biting, which was serving him well now as Scarlett launched into another tirade.

'This is meant to be our *anniversary*, Elliot!' she yelled, emphasising the occasion as if he could have somehow forgotten.

'Yes, I know it is. But you can hardly blame me for the traffic problems, Scarlett. Or the car breaking down. Or the mix-up with the hotel room.'

'How am I supposed to know it wasn't you who mixed up the rooms?' she asked, wrenching a phone charger from her suitcase and throwing it down on the bed. 'After all, it was you who booked it.'

Yes, because I'm the one who always does these things, Elliot thought. *Maybe if you got off your privileged backside and—* 'The receptionist said it was to do with their new computer system. Just one of those things.'

'Just one of those things,' Scarlett repeated, with mock laughter. 'Just like the car breaking down. Again.'

'And what do you want me to do about it now?' Elliot asked, trying desperately to keep a lid on his temper. 'It's been back in to the dealership three times now and they've said they can't find a fault.'

'Well maybe if we'd gone for the Mercedes instead, like I wanted, then we wouldn't have to keep taking it back to the bloody dealership, would we?' she replied, tugging her make-up bag loose from under Elliot's neatly folded shirts.

Elliot sighed. There was no point. They'd been over this a hundred times before. How, in fact, it was he who'd wanted the Mercedes but Scarlett had twisted his arm into buying the BMW. How he'd pointed out that the Mercedes would be more reliable but that Scarlett had preferred the interior on the BMW. How she was always bloody right, even when she was wrong.

'Is that it?' she said, thrusting her hands on her hips. 'A sigh?'

'What do you want me to say?' Elliot asked, hoping for some sort of tip as to how he could end this daft charade. After five years of marriage, though, he knew there was only one way.

'Nothing. There's nothing you can say.'

'Right. Well I'm going to the bar, then.'

2

'Large scotch, please,' Elliot said, the barman's permanent smile putting him on edge. He was never sure how to react when people were overly nice. Should he drop his defences and smile back, no matter how upset or annoyed he was, or should he allow it to infuriate him even more to the point where he wanted to punch him in the face? *Rise above it*, he told himself. He wasn't angry at the barman; he was angry at Scarlett.

He was amazed at how often he had to tell himself that. As far as he was concerned, it just went to show that Scarlett's attitude and behaviour had permeated every fibre of his being and was starting to affect so many different areas of his life. He wasn't one for confrontation, though, and preferred to keep things bottled up. That wasn't a problem, as he never stayed angry for long. At some point tonight he'd have calmed down, Scarlett would have just pretended the whole thing never happened, she'd flounce down to dinner, they'd have a bottle or two of wine, head back upstairs and... Well, she had her uses.

Right now, though, his attention was fixed firmly on the glass of scotch, for no other reason than to take his mind of the fact that he'd just paid twelve pounds for it. *Way to calm a man down*, he thought.

He sloshed the amber liquid around in his glass, clinking the ice off the side of the glass as it slowly melted, releasing the potent fumes of the whisky.

'Long day?' the barman asked as he wiped between the beer pumps with a cloth.

'Hmm? Oh. No, sorry,' Elliot said, waking himself from his stupor. 'Silly argument with my wife. Just one of those things.'

'Ah. I did wonder,' he said. 'Not often you get men drinking scotch at six o'clock in the evening.'

'No. Well, it'll be my only one, I suppose. Especially at these prices.'

The barman laughed a knowing laugh, as if he'd heard that line a few times before. 'Funny. You don't seem like the marrying type to me,' he said.

Elliot allowed himself to smile for the first time that evening. 'No. I'm starting to think that might be the case myself.'

TUESDAY 17TH MARCH

3

The comfort of the Freemason's Arms seemed like luxury to Ellis Flint. He was a firm believer that holidays were meant to be relaxing affairs, but the one he'd just returned from had been anything but.

'You two are bloody murder magnets from what I hear,' the landlord, Doug Lilley, said as he pulled on the pump to pour Ellis's pint. 'In fact, perhaps it's in my best interests that I bar you,' he added, laughing.

'I think you're safe,' Ellis said. 'Lightning never strikes twice.' Indeed, the very first murder that Ellis and his friend Kempston Hardwick had investigated had taken place in the Freemason's Arms a little over three years earlier.

'Bloody strikes constantly when you two are about,' Doug replied. 'Rate you're going, you'll turn this place into some sort of cheap detective series location.'

'Well, at least we're doing our bit for the community. I

can't see them closing down the police station if the murder rate stays this high.'

Tollinghill Police Station had been earmarked for closure by the county force in the previous few months as part of the present government's cost-cutting exercises. It was all about 'streamlining' and 'centralising services'. Once all of the corporate-speak had been cut through, the bottom line was that it came down to money. Liberty and safety had been reduced to mere commodities.

'Heh. Every cloud and all that,' Doug said, leaning in towards Ellis. 'Here, that reminds me. Did you hear about that bloke topping himself down at the Manor Hotel in South Heath last Thursday?'

'No,' Ellis said. 'What happened?'

'Hung himself from the rafters on the top floor. Nothing suspicious, like. Well, not officially, anyway. But it's a bit weird, ain't it, after all them stories about the ghosts and that?'

'Ghosts?' Ellis asked, his interest piqued. Ellis's interest in the paranormal had come to the fore on more than one occasion recently, and he was sure that many of the odd goings on in and around Tollinghill could be attributed to supernatural forces. He vaguely recalled a ghost story concerning the Manor Hotel but couldn't remember any details.

'Yeah, an old woman supposedly haunts it,' Doug said. 'Story goes, a child died there, back when it was a private manor, back in Victorian times. They reckon it was the nanny who had poisoned the young lad, and they sacked her on the spot even though she said she didn't do it. Few years later, the old dear dies in poverty and never got to clear her name. Legend has it that it's her ghost who still haunts the manor, trying to protest her innocence.'

Ellis felt the hairs on the back of his neck stand up and realised his breathing was becoming more and more shallow.

'Apparently it all kicked off when they converted it into a hotel,' Doug continued. 'The builders had been doing some renovation work and took some tiles off the roof. Turns out there was a secret hidden room on the top level, which no-one knew about. They reckon it's what would've been the servants' quarters. The room where the nanny would've lived. That's when it all started kicking off.'

'Kicking off?' Ellis asked.

'Well, they gradually turned the top floor rooms into more hotel rooms, as well as keeping a couple for the staff. Housekeepers and that. Few weeks later, people started seeing things. Couple of people reckon they saw an old woman sat at the end of their bed, crying. Quite a lot of footsteps coming from the room where she would've lived, too.'

'Sounds like a nice little bit of marketing to me,' Ellis said, not believing his own cynicism but trying desperately to come up with a rational explanation in order to stop himself getting completely spooked.

'That's where you're wrong, see. The hotel owners went and spoke to a couple of the families who lived there, back when it was in private hands. Turns out the previous owner said his mum used to hear someone knocking on her bedroom door at night, even if she was the only person there. And other people saw things, too.'

Ellis sat back and thought for a moment. 'Doug,' he said, leaning forward once more. 'What's this got to do with this bloke's suicide, exactly?'

'You tell me, Ellis,' Doug said, standing up and brushing down the bar with a cloth. 'You tell me.'

WEDNESDAY 18TH MARCH

4

'So what you're trying to tell me is that a non-existent spiritual being has somehow wrapped a rope around a chap's neck and left him swinging from the rafters in a hotel, yes?' Kempston Hardwick said, sounding completely serious but with that subtle tone of underlying sarcasm that Ellis had come to know so well.

'No, what I'm trying to say is that it's a good story,' Ellis said. 'It's interesting. All that weird stuff going on, and then a bloke goes and tops himself in the same room. Bit of a coincidence, isn't it?'

'Yes, Ellis. That's exactly what it is. A coincidence and a good story. Tell me, do you know how many people die in hotels every year? Thousands. Think how many people pass through a hotel in a year. And how many people must have stayed in that room? I hardly think one suicide is a worrying statistic. Besides, it was converted to a hotel nearly twenty years ago. It's hardly all happening at once, is it?'

'Things have been happening for years, Kempston. This is just the tip of the iceberg.'

'Who told you that?' Hardwick asked.

'Doug, at the Freemason's, last night,' Ellis replied.

'Ah yes. Doug Lilley. Award-winning licensee and master storyteller. You can't believe everything you're told, Ellis. Especially not in a place like Tollinghill. You should know that by now.'

'Ah, but that's not all. You said about how many people must've stayed in that room. This bloke, Elliot Carr, wasn't even staying in that room. He was staying in a suite on the room below with his wife. So why was he hanging from the rafters in room thirteen?'

'Room thirteen? Oh come on, Ellis. That's not even imaginative.'

'That's how many rooms there are, Kempston. Thirteen. It's on the top floor and they're numbered upwards. Hardly my fault. Anyway, why was he up there hanging from the rafters if he was staying down in room seven?'

'Does room seven have exposed rafters?' Hardwick asked.

'I don't know. I shouldn't think so,' Ellis said.

'There you go, then. Mystery solved. Mr Carr rightly deduced that he couldn't hang himself from an Artex ceiling and, in a moment of groundbreaking genius, went to the room with exposed rafters.'

'But why?' Ellis asked. 'He was there enjoying an anniversary break with his wife. They'd been married five years. Why would he want to kill himself?'

'I think you just answered that question, Ellis,' Hardwick replied. He'd never been one for marriage, or for any type of relationship or romance at all, for that matter. As far as Hardwick was concerned, romance and courtship were unnecessary distractions from the seriousness of life.

'I don't know, Kempston. It just doesn't seem right. According to Doug, Elliot Carr hung himself with a cord from one of the dressing gowns they keep in the storage room. He didn't take anything up to the room with him, so it doesn't sound like he planned it. He'd even set his alarm for the next morning. Why would you do that if you'd planned to kill yourself?'

'Perhaps it was a spur-of-the-moment thing,' Hardwick offered.

'What, so on the spur of the moment he just decided to walk up to the top floor where he happened to know there was an unoccupied room with exposed rafters and a handy dressing gown cord which he could hang himself with? Doesn't sound all that likely to me.'

Hardwick was silent for a few moments. 'No. Now that you put it like that, it doesn't sound too likely to me, either.'

'Go on,' Ellis said. 'What's the punchline?'

'Hmmm?'

'Well, I don't often manage to talk you round that

easily. I presume there must be some sarcastic comment or quip on its way at some point.'

'Not at all, Ellis,' Hardwick replied. 'In fact, I was just thinking about how easily you *do* manage to talk me round.'

5

Detective Inspector Rob Warner was not someone who liked having his time wasted. Although he'd had cause to call on Kempston Hardwick's assistance and expertise in the past, he largely found him an irritation, more often than not getting in the way of his own investigational procedures.

Indeed, it was only recently that he'd had to bail Hardwick out of a Greek prison after Hardwick had been unable to manage even a week's holiday without getting himself muddled up in a murder case. He presumed Hardwick must have his reasons for being constantly compelled to get involved, but as far as Warner was concerned it was just another added complication that he didn't need.

With the police service having to work around stringent budget cuts at the present time, enlisting the help of outside contractors was not high on the agenda. Rather infuriatingly for DI Warner, this was not a reason he could use for keeping Kempston Hardwick at arms' length, as Hardwick never charged for his services.

This had always intrigued Warner. Try as he might — and he had — he could never find out anything about who Kempston Hardwick really was. How he earned a living. Where he came from before he moved to Tollinghill. Whether he had any family. This, in itself, had made him more than a little suspicious of Hardwick over the years, although he could never quite pin anything on him.

Muscling in on murder investigations was one thing, but Hardwick trying to convince him that a cut-and-dried suicide was actually a murder was something else entirely.

'The pathologist's report was pretty clear, Hardwick,' Warner said, getting straight to the point as he always did. 'Witnesses saw Elliot Carr speaking about the argument he'd had with his wife and an hour or two later he topped himself. It's a straightforward suicide.'

'A little too straightforward,' Hardwick replied.

DI Warner sat back in his chair, interlocked his fingers across his stomach and exhaled deeply. 'Go on,' he said, having by now realised that he would have to at least humour Hardwick if he was ever going to get home tonight.

'Am I right in thinking that Elliot Carr went down to the hotel bar and had a couple of drinks between the argument and his death?' Hardwick asked.

'Who told you that?' Warner asked, his eyes narrowing. 'You do realise that this is a police case and that certain details are confidential, don't you?'

'What's confidential?' Hardwick replied. 'I know Elliot Carr was in the bar that night because a number of people saw him. He was staying over at the hotel and I assumed he would have been drinking alcohol. Especially if he was in the frame of mind which might have driven him towards killing himself, which you suspect.'

'Yes. It seems as though the alcohol might have pushed him over the edge,' Warner said.

'And am I also right in thinking that the witnesses in the bar that night said that he seemed to be in brighter spirits when he left the bar than when he arrived?'

Warner started to ask Hardwick where he was getting this information from, then thought better of it. 'Yes, you often find that with suicides. The final acceptance, the moment of clarity.'

'Indeed. And rather than walking two hundred yards to the mainline railway or heading for the river that runs behind the hotel, or indeed even for any one of the number of wooded copses, he went upstairs to the top floor of the hotel — a floor he'd never set foot on in a hotel he'd never been to, went into a room he knew would not only have exposed rafters and corded dressing gowns stored there but also be unoccupied, and ended his life there?'

'Hardwick, I'm not sure what you're getting at here but I think I can guess. You can't just go around seeing murder mysteries everywhere. Life doesn't work like that,' Warner said, crossing his arms.

'Would it not be a little more prudent to investigate the

possibilities instead of the alternative option of potentially letting a killer run free?'

Warner sighed and dropped his chin against his chest. 'Listen to me. There *is* no killer because there *was* no murder. Elliot Carr committed suicide. The scenes of crime officers said it, the pathologist said it and, more importantly, I said it. Now, if you'll excuse me,' he added, standing and ushering Hardwick towards the door, 'I've got more important business to be getting on with.'

'More important than murder? Tell me, is it the pen pushing or doughnut eating?'

DI Warner looked daggers at Hardwick. 'You're pushing your luck now. Leave.'

6

Kit Daniels drummed frantically on his desk as the pen bounced up and down, pivoting between his index and middle fingers, sighing as the fingernails on his other hand scratched at the stubble which had begun to grow on his chin.

It was always the same. The Tollinghill Echo was run almost solely on the basis that it needed sensationalist stories in order to make money by selling up to the nationals, yet his editor, Sally Marsh, seemed to be less than enthusiastic about yet another one of his stories.

Apparently a mysterious and rather suspicious suicide just wasn't enough for Sally, despite the fact that this one looked particularly dodgy and could well turn out to be something other than suicide. That's if the local fuzz ever pulled their fingers out and actually looked at the facts, of course.

He sighed again and decided that he'd give it one last

go. Picking up his notebook, he pushed his chair back on its casters and walked over towards Sally's office. Peering through the window between the venetian blinds he could see that she wasn't on the phone but was instead passively engaged in something on her computer. Probably another game of *Solitaire*, he thought. He knocked, waited for an answer and entered.

'Sally, I just wanted to speak to you again about this death at the Manor Hotel,' Kit said, as pleasantly as he could manage.

'The suicide, you mean?' Sally replied, raising an eyebrow as she did so.

'The suspicious suicide, yes.'

'Suspicious according to you, Kit.'

'With respect, Sally, it's my job to investigate stories and find the truth. And I think there's a whole other truth underneath this one. If there's something big here we could sell it up to the nationals and make some decent money.'

'And if there isn't?' Sally replied, barely taking her eyes off the computer screen.

'Then what have we lost, Sally? A few column inches?'

'If only it were that simple. Column inches cost money. Not only that, but if you engage on some sort of personal mission to uncover secrets which don't exist you'll end up upsetting the family and the police, which'll not only jeopardise our chances of getting decent information in the future but it could end up costing us money in court cases.'

'Only if we say something which isn't true,' Kit replied. 'Anyway, that's never stopped us before.'

'I'm not quite sure what you're getting at, Kit,' Sally said, taking her attention off the screen and making eye contact with him for the first time that day. 'Every story we publish goes through me. Every word is scrutinised and if I don't believe it'll stand up then I won't publish it.'

'Every word?'

'Every word.'

'Are you sure about that?' Kit asked.

'If I were you, I wouldn't go throwing accusations around. This is a carefully constructed business model and it's one which works.'

'Business model?' Kit barked, almost exploding with rage. 'This is meant to be a newspaper!'

'Newspapers have to make money, Kit,' Sally replied, keeping a calm and level head as she always did. Often she was far too calm and laid-back for situations and this tended to enrage people even more. 'Listen, I know you're stressed out at the moment and the changes coming from on high aren't helping anybody. But the best thing we can do is to function as a unit. Yes, we need sensational stories. But there's nothing sensational about a suicide in a hotel.'

'Even if the deceased happened to be perfectly happy and had no reason to kill themselves?'

'You never know what's going through a person's mind. It's often the seemingly happiest and cheeriest people who are actually at their lowest ebb. The tears of the clown, Kit. So to answer your question, no, I don't think this story's big enough to run. If there were to be another death, of course, then we'd be talking serious money.'

THURSDAY 19TH MARCH

7

'I knew you'd find it a bit weird,' Ellis said as he tried to keep up with Hardwick's fast pace. 'I mean, it must've made you realise something was up when I mentioned how odd it was.'

'My suspicions were confirmed when I spoke to DI Warner, Ellis. My general rule in life is to do the complete opposite of what he does. It usually works.'

'What was all that stuff about the witnesses, though? I didn't think you'd spoken to anyone at the hotel that night.'

'I haven't. But if I was wrong then DI Warner would have corrected me. Which he didn't. Which means I was right.'

'That'll make a nice change,' Ellis muttered to himself as he stumbled to keep up.

'Which is why I want to get down there and speak to the witnesses while I still can,' Hardwick called over his shoulder as he strode forward.

'Do we really need to walk it, though?' Ellis asked, occasionally breaking into a jog. The walk to the Manor Hotel in South Heath was around three miles from Hardwick's home at the Old Rectory in Tollinghill. Although Tollinghill and South Heath were divided only by a roundabout and a dual carriageway, both the Old Rectory and the Manor Hotel were on the far sides of each town, which had only become conjoined owing to fairly modern housing developments.

'Walking clears the mind, Ellis. It helps me think freely. Besides, you could do with a bit of exercise.'

'Oh, charming, that is. Could we not have just got a bus?'

'We can walk it in around forty-five minutes if we're brisk. We'd have to wait half an hour for a bus as it is, then another half an hour while it drives around all the housing estates one by one, only to be dropped off half an hour's walk from the Manor anyway. So no.'

'Do you always have to get your own way?' Ellis asked in between pants and gasps.

Hardwick's reply was brief. 'Yes.'

As they approached the southern outskirts of South Heath, Hardwick marched up the long, sweeping drive that led to the Manor Hotel, Ellis limping and mumbling behind him.

'You know, I've never actually been here,' Hardwick said, stopping suddenly, his feet scuffing to a halt on the gravel. 'In all the time I've lived in Tollinghill, I've never actually walked up here.'

'Me neither,' Ellis said. 'Nice, though.'

'Such a way with words, Ellis.'

The gravel drive was around two hundred metres long, itself a spur off the very quiet and secluded Manor Drive, which swept up the side of the old manor grounds that now formed twenty-two hectares of public space and was home to all manner of wildlife.

'I've been doing a bit of research, actually,' Ellis said. Despite his regular intellectual shortcomings, Ellis had a habit of being a keen researcher.

'Let me guess,' Kempston said, pre-empting him. 'Ghosts and ghoulies?'

'No, actually,' Ellis replied. 'When the manor was bought and turned into a hotel, they had some renovation work done. Something to do with the roof. Apparently, when the builders took the tiles off the roof, they discovered an attic room which wasn't visible from inside the manor. They reckon it would've once been one of the servants' rooms. Why it was then walled up is anyone's guess. Anyway, that's when strange things started happening.'

'It was only a matter of time,' Hardwick said, sighing.

'What?'

'Before you started talking about ghosts and paranormal activity. You're utterly predictable, Ellis.'

'I'm just telling you what I've read, Kempston. Now, may I continue?' Hardwick said nothing, so he did. 'A couple of nights later, the receptionist, who was staying in one of the hotel rooms, woke up and saw an old woman in her room. She jumped out of bed screaming and left the room. When she came back, the lights were on, even though she hadn't turned them on.'

'Cowboy electricians for you,' Hardwick remarked. Ellis ignored him.

'She said the old woman was crying and she was obviously extremely upset. Not long after that, a guest at the hotel woke up when he heard a shuffling sound at the bottom of his bed. When he switched his light on, there was an old woman stood there, looking out of the window. He spoke to her but she didn't reply. Then she just faded away.'

'And who, pray tell, is this woman supposed to be?' Hardwick asked, humouring him.

'Well, that's the interesting thing. Back in Victorian times, there was a bit of a scandal at the manor. The live-in nanny was an older woman who was accused of trying to poison one of the children. The family sacked her, despite her protesting her innocence. The child died a few weeks later. As it happens, they reckon that the room the builders uncovered would've probably been the nanny's room.'

'So what,' Kempston said. 'They've just "unlocked" her ghost?'

'Yes. Exactly. What other explanations are there?' Ellis asked.

'Many, Ellis. Many.'

. . .

The inside of the Manor Hotel was just as magnificent as the outside. An antique writing desk sat jauntily adjacent to the edge of the reception area, an ornate Edwardian chair behind it and a reading lamp on top of it. A large, sweeping staircase, bedecked with a deep red carpet, beckoned visitors from the parquet-floored reception to the higher levels of the manor. It looked more like the hallway of a mansion than a hotel.

A woman, Mandy according to her name badge, greeted Hardwick and Flint as they entered.

'Good afternoon, gentlemen. Can I help?'

'Yes, we were just wondering if we might be able to try your famous afternoon teas,' Hardwick said, getting in quickly before Ellis opened his mouth with questions about ghosts and spectres.

'Of course. The lounge room is just through that door on your left. If you carry on through, there'll be someone there to greet you.'

Hardwick and Flint did as they were told and walked through to the lounge room. A collection of ornate paintings hung on the walls, with display cabinets showing off all manner of ornaments. To one side, a bar area presented an impressive array of malt whiskies and other spirits.

The lounge area was devoid of people other than the woman working behind the bar, who was at that moment busy trying to get to grips with the coffee machine. Hardwick waited a few moments before clearing his throat.

'Oh, sorry!' the woman said, startled at having only just

realised she had company. 'Trying to get this bloody thing to work. Can I help you at all?'

'Sorry, didn't mean to startle you,' Ellis said, before Hardwick had a chance to speak. 'Don't worry, we're not ghosts.'

The woman raised one eyebrow as Hardwick cut in. 'Yes, we were just wondering if we might have a coffee, actually,' Hardwick said, sensing that this might keep her occupied for a little longer, allowing him to ask more questions.

'Well, I'll try,' she said. Hardwick noted her name — Barbara — from her name badge. 'Fact is, we're a little short staffed at the moment. The lad who usually works behind the bar just upped and left last Thursday.'

'Thursday?' Hardwick asked, his ears pricking up.

'Yeah, just disappeared. Can't trust these young lads. They don't like hard work, see.'

'Wasn't there an incident here last Thursday?' Hardwick asked. 'I think I saw something in the newspaper.'

'Ah, yes. The *suicide*,' Barbara said, whispering the word in a conspiratorial manner. 'Nasty business. Happens in hotels more often than you'd think, though.'

'So I hear,' Hardwick said. 'Were you working that night?'

'Oh yes, I'm always working. Glutton for punishment, me,' Barbara replied, allowing herself a small chuckle.

'What's your job title?' Ellis asked.

'Job title? Heh. I don't have a job title, love. Well, I suppose I'm technically a housekeeper. I do all sorts.

Sometimes the bar, sometimes a bit on reception. Generally making sure the place runs smoothly, really. On paper I'm a nobody, but everyone in the hotel trade knows who keeps these places running and it isn't the directors or the managers, you know,' she said, with cheeky smile, a wink and a tap on her nose.

'I'm sure you do a marvellous job,' Hardwick said. 'Have you worked here long?'

'Shortly after it opened as a hotel, about seventeen years ago. Doesn't give me much time off, but then again I never married and I'm perfectly happy spending my time here. Certainly better than having a mortgage.'

'Must be busy work,' Ellis said, looking around the room.

'Oh yes, it certainly is. I get some time off in the evenings sometimes and on Sundays I go and help out at the church. Volunteering, you know.'

'Lovely,' Ellis replied. 'Have you always done this sort of thing then?'

'Oh no. I used to be a lawyer, actually. Back when there weren't many female lawyers. Working in the hotel business might seem like hard work, but it's nothing compared to that.'

'Glad you got out of it?' Ellis asked.

'Oh, yes. I'd say so. It might have been an achievement to get that far but it was pretty clear that a lot of the old boys' club didn't want a woman knocking around and ruining things for them. I took early retirement after a few years and decided to do something totally different. And you don't get much more different than this. Ooh!' she said, suddenly remembering. 'You wanted coffee, didn't you?'

'Please, if it's not too much trouble,' Hardwick said, before adding, to fill the silence, 'It's a lovely place, isn't it. The manor.'

'Oh yes. Beautiful.'

'Any ghosts?' Ellis said. Hardwick looked daggers at him. Barbara chuckled to herself.

'Well, many people would say so. I don't know how much I believe it myself, but there are a few stories, yes.'

'Do you know anything about them?' Ellis asked.

'Not in detail, no. A few of the locals could probably tell you. I try to avoid that sort of thing, if I'm honest. Although there are sometimes some odd things that happen.'

'Oh?' Ellis asked, leaning forward on the bar.

'Well, just noises and things really. Sometimes I hear footsteps at night. My room is on the middle floor, see. Not all the rooms are guest rooms. As we're a bit remote there are some rooms set aside for staff, particularly the full-time ones. Someone mentioned something about insurance and health and safety things if you've got more than a certain number of guest rooms. Not exactly that easy to stick a disabled lift in a building of this age, you know. I suppose by having some of the full-time staff living in, they're able to pay them less too. Living allowance, or whatever. As I say, the money's not really a concern for me. I've always lived frugally and earned more than my keep when I was in the law game.'

'But have you heard anything... out of the ordinary?' Ellis asked, wanting to get some juicy ghost stories far more than he wanted to hear Barbara's life story.

'I quite often hear what sounds like someone walking around in the room above.'

'Would that be room thirteen by any chance?' Hardwick asked, by now quite keen on the idea of a coffee.

'Yes. Yes, it is. It's very rarely booked in, to be honest. It used to be used as an overflow room but we tend to find that guests aren't very keen on it for some reason. Something to do with an oppressive atmosphere. As a general rule, it's just used as a storage room now.'

'And this was the room Elliot Carr committed suicide in, wasn't it?' Hardwick asked.

'Yes. How did you know that?' Barbara replied.

'The newspaper report said something about him hanging himself from the exposed rafters. I supposed that could only be the case on the top floor.'

'Yes, that's true,' Barbara said. 'Terrible thing, that. He seemed like such a nice chap.'

'You met him?' Hardwick asked.

'Oh yes, of course. He was down here in the bar earlier that evening.'

'Did he say much?'

'Not really,' Barbara said. 'To be honest, I was darting about sorting out lots of different things, as usual. One minute on the bar, the next helping move stuff in the store cupboard, then seeing to new arrivals, making coffee... Oh, coffee!' she exclaimed as she darted an index finger upwards.

Hardwick gave her a few moments to actually head in the direction of the coffee machine before he started talking again. 'Did you hear what he was talking about at all?'

'Not really, no. Something about an argument with his wife. Didn't seem too serious, but you never know, do you?'

'Indeed not,' Hardwick replied, noting that she had once again moved away from the coffee machine without even pressing a button. 'And did you see Mrs Carr at all?'

'No, I didn't, actually. I saw them both when they arrived, and then after the police had been I assumed she had gone with them, or back home or wherever. I don't know. I wasn't always around. As I said, Owen Bartlett was on the bar all night. That's the lad who used to work here. He'd know more. He was speaking to him for quite a long time.'

'And that's the chap who disappeared later that night?' Hardwick asked.

'Yes,' Barbara replied, her voice now much more serious. 'That's him.'

As Hardwick and Flint left the lounge and bar area and headed back through to the reception and front entrance, Mandy was stood by the antique reception table, ready to offer more of her fawning, false *yes-sir-thankyou-sir* hospitality.

'Everything okay for you, gentlemen?' she asked with a plastered grin.

'Yes, absolutely lovely. Thank you,' Hardwick said, before stopping in his tracks and putting his hand to his head. 'Damn!' he said. 'I've only gone and left my wallet on the bar.'

'No worries, sir,' Mandy said, already on her way. 'I'll just go and fetch it for you. Won't be a moment.'

Before Ellis could even fathom what was going on, Hardwick had shot round to the other side of the table and was thumbing furiously through the bookings book. Fortunately for him, the Manor Hotel was sufficiently keen on maintaining its style to have stuck with the traditional pen and paper arrangements instead of investing in a computer system.

'72 Trinity Crescent, Bellingham,' Hardwick said, committing the address to memory. 'Come on Ellis, let's go.'

'What? Whose address is that?' Ellis asked as Hardwick marched past him and through the front door.

'Elliot and Scarlett Carr's, Ellis. Do keep up.'

8

The pair had barely walked half a mile up the main road in South Heath before Ellis insisted they stop at the Dove, a pub which sat alongside the railway bridge which connected east and west sides of South Heath, which were otherwise split by the mainline railway into London.

The pub was a traditional two-bar affair, with a hard-floored saloon bar containing a pool table and darts board as well as a spacious carpeted lounge room. Ellis, never one to worry about the social niceties of whether it was too early to drink, ordered a pint of the local beer from up the road in Shafford. Hardwick, having been quite looking forward to his ultimately elusive cup of coffee in the Manor Hotel, opted for a caffeine fix.

'So what are you saying? You're just going to march down to see the grieving widow and interrogate her?' Ellis asked. 'What good will that do?'

'We need to find out more about her husband, Ellis.

The first step of any murder investigation is to find out about the victim. You should know this by now.'

'But we don't know that there has been a murder or a victim. Shouldn't we be a bit more careful?' Ellis asked, by now having already downed half his pint.

'Ellis, it might have escaped your notice that it was you who tried to convince me that something wasn't quite right about Elliot Carr's *suicide*,' Hardwick said, stressing the word with invisible speech marks. 'You can't go backing down now. What if he was killed? Now, we have to consider all possibilities, don't we?'

'I didn't mean that it had to be a murder, though, did I? I was looking more at the paranormal side of things. There's a lot of weird things gone on at that place over the years, you know.'

Hardwick ignored this comment and blew across his mug of coffee as Ellis downed another mouthful of beer.

'As I see it, there are quite a few possibilities,' Hardwick continued. 'Yes, Elliot Carr may well have killed himself. That's the official line and it's one we must consider. However, we also have a few complications. Aside from the practicalities that you brought to my attention, there's also an upset and angry wife.'

'How do you know she was upset and angry?' Ellis asked. 'We've not even spoken to her yet.'

'Elliot Carr said to the barman himself they'd just had an argument, Ellis. Even though he had cheered up somewhat by the end of the evening, no doubt Mrs Carr would've stayed angry and upset.' *Because she's a woman,*

Ellis knew Hardwick was thinking but wouldn't dare say. 'Besides, it's difficult to ignore the fact that Owen Bartlett, who had been working behind the bar and had got to know Mr Carr that night, disappeared without trace on the night Mr Carr died. Does that not strike you as a bit odd?'

'Well, yes. But he might have just got spooked. You know what young lads can be like,' Ellis replied.

'Oh yes, I do. And we need to speak to him.'

'How?' Ellis asked. 'I mean, there must be a record of his address somewhere, but God knows how we'd get it. Not the sort of thing that'd just be written down at the reception desk like the Carrs' address, is it?'

'No, it certainly isn't. I might need to have a think on that one,' Hardwick said. 'In the meantime, we should head down to Bellingham and speak to Mrs Carr.'

'When?' Ellis asked.

'No time like the present, Ellis,' came the reply.

'Well, I can't go back and get the car. I've just downed a pint.'

'Good job we're right next to the train station, then, isn't it?'

Before Ellis had a chance to reply, Hardwick had drunk his mug of coffee in one go, stood up and headed for the door.

9

The train journey to Bellingham had been a fairly straight-forward one, being only twenty minutes or so further down the line towards London. Bellingham was firmly in the commuter belt, being far enough outside London to not be considered London but close enough for the house prices to be immorally high.

It was a fifteen minute walk from the train station to 72 Trinity Crescent. The area was pleasant enough, but had a certain air of stuffiness about it. Hardwick was sure he knew the types who lived here: soulless career-oriented commuters and their stay-at-home wives, sipping skinny lattes in the town's boutique coffee houses before hopping into the Range Rover to pick up little Tarquin and Polly from school.

Hardwick had never been one for pretension, as much as people thought they detected it in him. Ellis, however, was in his element.

'Cor, wouldn't you just love to live in a place like this, Kempston?'

'I'm quite happy where I am, Ellis, thank you.'

'No, but I mean, these people are really going places.'

'They're going to work, Ellis. They go to work, they come home. They're trapped in a life of soulless drudgery. So to answer your question, no, I would not like to live in a place like this.'

As they rounded the corner onto Trinity Crescent, Hardwick glanced at the house numbers, trying to ascertain where number 72 would be.

'What are they? Four bedrooms? Five?' Ellis asked.

'Number 72 has four bedrooms,' Hardwick replied, having already done his research using Ellis's smartphone while they waited for their train.

'Blimey. Must be worth half a million quid around here.'

'It sold for 1.2 million, two and a half years ago,' Hardwick replied. 'Worth around 1.4 now.'

'Jesus! For four bedrooms? Your place must be worth at least that, then,' Ellis said.

'I don't know and I don't care, Ellis,' Hardwick said. 'Because I have no intention of moving. And anyway, I live in Tollinghill, not Bellingham. Thankfully.'

As they reached number 72, Hardwick strolled purposefully up the short driveway, a BMW parked in front of the bay window, hidden from the road by the hedge that separated the front garden from the road.

Before Ellis had even set foot on the driveway, Hardwick had pressed his finger on the doorbell.

A few moments later, a man aged around sixty opened the door, his glasses perched on the end of his nose.

'Ah, sorry,' Ellis said, as he arrived at the door. 'I think we've got the wrong house.'

'Hello. Is this where Mrs Scarlett Carr lives?' Hardwick asked, ignoring Ellis.

'Yes, it is,' the man replied. 'Can I help you?'

'Yes, we'd just like to have a quick chat with Mrs Carr, if we may. Regarding the death of her husband.'

'Ah, I see. Come in then,' the man said, ushering them through into the hallway. 'Scarlett? The police want a word again,' he said as he put his head through into the living room.

Ellis was quick to respond. 'Oh, we're not—'

'Not going to take up much of your time,' Hardwick interrupted, treading on Ellis's foot. 'Just a few things the coroner's court want us to clarify before they can proceed.'

'Oh. Yes, of course. Sorry about the mess,' Scarlett said, gesturing to the papers and documents strewn across the coffee table. 'Dad and I have been going through all the paperwork. Bank accounts and things. It's never-ending. Helps with the grieving process, I suppose. Keeps my mind occupied.' Her voice cracked slightly as she spoke.

'Well we won't take up much of your time,' Hardwick said, sitting down on the leather sofa as Scarlett's father hovered by the doorway. 'First of all, you and your husband had an argument on the night of his death. Is that right?'

'Uh, yes,' Scarlett said, blinking. 'But I've already told the other officers this a number of times.'

'We just need to make sure we have everything noted down for ourselves,' Hardwick replied with a smile. 'I'm sure you can understand.'

'Well, yes. And yes, we did. Just another silly thing, really. The car broke down on the way there. Again. And there'd been a mix-up with the hotel rooms. We were both stressed and it turned into an argument, but nothing serious.'

'Did your husband handle stressful situations well, Mrs Carr?' Ellis asked.

'Well, yes. I think so. He tended to keep things bottled up. He didn't really talk about what was upsetting him, if things were. That probably makes it worse, doesn't it? You always hear about people who soak up stress like a sponge, but all that energy and tension has to go somewhere. It just coils up like a spring, until one day...' She trailed off and wiped an eye.

'It uncoils,' Hardwick said. 'And did you have any inkling that your husband might be the type to take his own life?'

'No. Not really. I mean, you never really know, do you? They say it's always the ones you least suspect. But you'd think a wife would know her husband, wouldn't you? That I'd've been able to spot the signs? I sometimes wonder if it was my fault.' Scarlett's father handed her a box of tissues from the sideboard as she sobbed into her hands.

'If you don't mind me being intrusive, Mrs Carr, what

had your husband's state of mind been like up until his death?' Hardwick asked.

'He'd been stressed with work, but aren't most people?' she said. Seeing Hardwick's raised eyebrow, she elaborated. 'He works in London, as a purchasing director at an art gallery. I think the recession's been tough for them. People are tightening their belts, even in the city. Plus there are new galleries, new competition, popping up all the time.'

'Yes, the recession has caused a lot of problems in the past few years,' Hardwick said, seeming to sympathise. 'When did you buy this house, Mrs Carr?'

'Uh, about two and a half years ago. Why?'

'Well, that was a good three or so years into the recession, wasn't it? Wasn't money already tight at that point?'

'I don't know,' Scarlett replied, breaking Hardwick's gaze. 'It was always Elliot who dealt with the money side of things. As you can see,' she said, gesturing again to the paperwork. 'It's a nightmare trying to get it all sorted out now. We'd been talking about moving for a while and one day I saw this place advertised in the window of an estate agent's in town. I fell in love with it straight away and knew we had to buy it.'

I bet you did, thought Hardwick. She struck him as the sort of woman who not only knew exactly what she wanted, but made sure she got it too. 'I see,' he said. 'Going back to the night Mr Carr died, could you talk me through what happened? You mentioned an argument, but what happened after?'

Scarlett put her hands together and interlocked her fingers. 'He did what he always did. He wouldn't do confrontation, so he went down to the bar. I stayed in the room and put the TV on.'

'What did you watch?' Hardwick asked.

'I don't know. Lots of things. I think there were a couple of quiz shows on. I just flicked through the channels trying to keep myself occupied.'

'Did you not think to go down after him?' Ellis said.

'No, there's no point. It was always best just to let things calm down. It's happened plenty of times before. Sooner or later he'd come back and apologise and everything was fine. I just sat in the room and waited.'

'And your room was on the middle floor, is that right?'

'Yes, room seven.'

'At what point did you go down to find him?' Ellis asked.

'I didn't. I think I must have fallen asleep in front of the TV. The next thing I knew, a policeman was knocking on the door of our room. That was when I... When he...'

Hardwick put her out of her misery. 'Yes, I see. And who found your husband?'

'Uh, one of the staff at the hotel, apparently. They were using the room for storage, they said. Towels and linen and things. Someone went in to get something and...' Scarlett trailed off and began to sob.

10

Kit Daniels was looking forward to getting home and kicking off his shoes to settle down in front of the TV. His parents would be out tonight so he'd at least be spared their nagging about him moving out and getting his own place.

They just didn't seem to understand that the world of journalism wasn't all about the big scoops and the huge payoffs. Most of it was dull, boring drudgery with absolutely no money in it at all. Constantly chasing the big story was all he could do, and it'd been a while since he'd hit a big scoop.

He'd had his big stories in the past, but they'd come quite quickly and regularly so he hadn't spent his bonuses all that wisely. A new car in the form of an Audi TT had waved goodbye to his first major bonus and taxing and insuring it had used up most of his salary since then.

Meeting Becky hadn't helped, either. That wasn't to say that he didn't love her — of course he loved her — but her constant nagging at him to settle down and get a place together hadn't helped. He was getting flak from all sides.

He wanted to settle down and move out but the money just wasn't there. His basic salary was keeping him going from month to month but not much else. His parents had suggested he sell the TT, but there wouldn't be a lot of point. It wasn't worth a whole lot any more — especially considering he'd have to buy another car anyway just to get to work — and he'd only be saving a fairly small amount each month, which'd be hardly worth it. No, he was far better off having his small luxuries and keeping his head high so he could work towards the next big scoop which would see him home and dry.

The heavy front door to the offices of the Tollinghill Echo seemed heavier than usual as he pushed it open and walked out into the chilly evening air.

'Kit!' came the familiar voice from the other side of the road. Becky. 'I thought I might see you. I was just on my way home myself.'

Sure you were, he thought. She knew damn well he had the house to himself and had planned to spend the evening alone. Just one night of peace and quiet. That's all he wanted.

'You don't usually come home this way, do you?' Kit asked, knowing full well that the walk home from the hair salon she worked in wouldn't take her anywhere near the Echo's offices.

'I walked Yvonne home. Her car broke down and, well, you know what she's like.'

Nope, he didn't. He'd heard Becky talking about Yvonne as he'd heard her talking about all sorts of things from the salon, but he'd never actually *listened*. Most of it went in one ear and out the other. Stories of how Mrs McArthur's dog got run over by a truck, how the new brand of hair dye they'd bought in had turned out to be rubbish. The usual stuff which Becky was quite convinced should be the new national scandal that Kit could break through the Tollinghill Echo.

'I was thinking perhaps we could do something together tonight,' she said. 'Didn't you say your parents were out? Perhaps we could watch a film or something. Or even go online and have a look at houses. What do you think?'

Kit sighed as he felt the familiar and comforting outline of the Audi's key fob in his jacket pocket.

'Yeah. Sure. Why not?'

11

On the train back to South Heath, Hardwick had phoned DI Warner (from Ellis's phone, of course) to ask the name of the person who'd found Elliot Carr's body. In an attempt to shut Hardwick up and stop him from finding out using his own methods, DI Warner told him it was Derren Robson, and it was him that Hardwick and Flint were on their way to see as Hardwick marched down the main road towards the Manor Hotel with Flint following not so closely behind him.

On arriving, the pair were greeted once again by Mandy, who seemed to be constantly working, overseeing her kingdom at the front desk.

'Hello again, gentlemen. Can I help?'

'We'd like to speak to Derren Robson, if we may, please.'

'Okay, can I ask what it's about?' Mandy asked,

cocking her head to the side and not letting her plastic smile drop for one moment.

'Yes, it's about the death of a guest last Thursday. We believe it was he who found the body.'

'Oh. Oh, yes, that's right,' she replied, the first sign of her smile dropping and her real face showing through. 'Sorry, I had no idea earlier that you were police officers.'

Hardwick looked at Flint and didn't say a word, but his face said it all. Flint opted not to speak.

Mandy led them through into the lounge room and went off to find Derren Robson. When they returned, Derren sat down on the plush sofa opposite Hardwick and Flint.

'Mr Robson, my name's Kempston Hardwick and this is my associate, Ellis Flint.' Derren's eyes seemed to flicker with a hint of recognition at their names, but Hardwick gave the man's brain no time to click into gear. 'I understand it was you who found the body of Elliot Carr last Thursday, is that correct?'

'Uh yes, it is. I went into room thirteen to grab some towels late that night. We put fresh linen in the public toilets regularly. Much nicer than paper towels or electric hand driers.' Hardwick didn't disagree. 'When I walked in, it was the first thing I saw. He was just dangling there, staring right at me, in the middle of the room.' Derren's face turned white and his jaw started to tremble as he spoke.

'And had you seen Mr Carr before this?' Ellis asked.

'Only around the hotel and at the bar that evening. I think he'd only arrived that afternoon.'

'What's your job title, Mr Robson?' Hardwick asked, changing tack quickly and effectively — a strategy he often employed to keep control of an interview.

'Job title? Well, I don't know. I was employed as a housekeeper, but I'm technically a concierge, I suppose. On paper I think it's "Hospitality Assurance Executive" or something like that. I don't know why they have to give stupid corporate titles to everything.'

Hardwick sensed a kindred spirit. 'What were your duties, though?'

'Oh, all sorts. We all kind of chip in and do everything, really. Some of us have things we prefer doing more than others, which works quite nicely. Some people like being on the bar and talking to customers. There are even people who like cleaning, believe it or not. I just get my head down and do what needs doing. It's a job at the end of the day.'

'An admirable stance,' Hardwick said. 'And is there a rota for changing the linen in the lavatories or do you wait until you're asked?'

'Bit of both, really. We try to do it three or four times a day. I think on Thursday night Barbara reminded me. To be honest, it was a good job she did. They didn't look like they'd been done since lunchtime.'

'I see. And did you notice anything odd at all that evening? Either about Mr Carr, his wife, or anyone else in the bar?'

'No, not really. Not at all actually. I didn't really spend much time around the bar area. To be honest, you'd probably be better off speaking to Owen Bartlett. He was on the bar that night.'

'Did he not disappear shortly after?' Ellis asked.

'He left, yeah.'

'Left?' Hardwick enquired.

'Yeah. I was in the reception area when he went. To be honest, he'd seemed a bit unhappy with the job for a while. He said this wasn't the sort of place he wanted to work and he was off.'

'Does that happen often?' Hardwick asked. 'People just walking out of their job?'

'Oh yes. More often than you'd think,' Derren replied.

'I see. Well, thank you for your time,' Hardwick said. 'Just one more thing, though. Could you please call us a taxi to take us to Tollinghill? It's getting late and it's a bit of a long walk.'

'Yes, of course,' Derren replied, slipping back into work mode. 'But I thought they were closing the police station up there? Thought they'd moved all your lot over to Shafford.'

Hardwick smiled and said nothing.

FRIDAY 20TH MARCH

12

Ellis Flint called round to the Old Rectory at nine o'clock
on Friday morning. He yawned as he knocked and waited
for Hardwick to answer. It had now been just over a week
since Elliot Carr had died and barely forty-eight hours
after Ellis had first told him about it, and sleep was the last
thing on Hardwick's mind, having been up all night
mulling over the known facts in his head.

'Come in, come in,' Hardwick said, gesturing for Ellis
to head on through to the kitchen. A pot of steaming coffee
was sat under the percolator, the deep brown liquid drip-
dripping into the pot. 'I've been awake most of the night,
actually, Ellis,' Hardwick said, spotting Ellis salivating over
the pot of coffee. 'Have a mug if you like. It's good stuff.'

Ellis poured himself a mug of coffee and sat at the
wooden kitchen table. It was then that he noticed possibly
the most baffling and extraordinary sight he'd witnessed in
the past few years. Kempston Hardwick had a laptop.

'Oh, don't look so surprised, Ellis. Needs must. Now, I've been doing a little bit of research. Have you ever heard of this thing called Facebook?'

Ellis looked aghast at Hardwick. 'Well yes. Of course I have.'

'Dreadful, isn't it? Quite handy, though. Yes, last night I spent some time setting up a Facebook profile.'

Ellis's eyes widened and he tried desperately to stifle a chuckle. He had visions of Hardwick's Facebook profile. *Relationship status: Single, very single. Hobbies and interests: Everything and nothing. Religious views: Don't ask.* 'Not a profile for myself, Ellis,' he said, almost reading his mind. 'For Sadie Brooks.'

'Who?' Ellis asked.

'Exactly. No-one. I made her up. Last night, after creating Sadie Brooks, I added Scarlett Carr as a friend. Predictably, she replied with a message asking who I was. I replied, as Sadie, that I was a work friend of Elliot's and that we'd met at a party a few months before. I guessed that Scarlett wouldn't be able to resist finding out more about Elliot's attractive work friend, so I sent her a link to a Facebook photo of Scarlett, Elliot and Sadie together at said party. Of course, the party and the photo never existed, nor did the link. The link went to a clone of Facebook which I'd created earlier, which asked her to log in to her account to view the photo. So Scarlett typed in her Facebook username and password, which was promptly emailed straight to me.'

'You... You hacked her Facebook account?' Ellis asked.

'No. She willingly gave up her login details, Ellis. She should have been more careful.'

'And when did you learn to do all this stuff? You didn't even have a computer yesterday morning!'

'It's really not difficult, Ellis. Why must you confuse things? As I was saying, her login details were emailed to me. I then logged out as Sadie and logged in using Scarlett's details. I knew something wasn't quite right about her, so I went straight to her messages. Turns out she hadn't been quite the faithful and dutiful wife she made out. Look at this,' Hardwick said, turning the laptop to face Ellis, who read the messages on the screen.

Scarlett: cant wait xx

Kevin: Me neither. you sure E hasn't cottoned on tho? X

Scarlett: he doesnt have the intelligence - brain like a puppet. were safe xx

'Who's Kevin?' Ellis asked.

'Kevin McGready,' Hardwick replied. 'Scarlett Carr's secret boyfriend. The messages go on for pages and pages and, quite frankly, they're nauseating. The upshot of it is that Scarlett had planned to leave Elliot and set up with this Kevin chap.'

'You're joking!' Ellis replied, lost for further words.

'I'm afraid not. Elliot Carr's death is starting to look rather more complicated than just a simple suicide, Ellis.'

13

When Hardwick and Flint arrived back at Scarlett Carr's house in Bellingham later that Friday morning, they were again greeted by her father at the door.

'I'm afraid she's not in,' the man said. 'She's in town at the moment, meeting a friend for coffee.'

Hardwick stood dumbstruck for a moment. He had never been one for sentimentality or emotion, but even he knew that the grieving process should probably last a little longer.

'I see,' he finally replied. 'And I just wondered if you could tell me, has a date been set for the funeral?'

'Yes, it'll be on Thursday 26th. Why?'

'Just procedure. And whereabouts is she meeting this friend? We need to have a quick word with her, if we may.'

'Well yes, of course,' he replied. 'She said she was going to Gianni's. It's on the Old Parade, just off the high street.'

Hardwick and Flint walked the three quarters of a mile back past the railway station, onto the high street and up Old Parade, a quaint pedestrianised area of the town filled with boutique clothes shops and cafés — here called 'tea rooms' or 'gourmet coffee houses', as was their pretentious bent.

They spotted Scarlett almost immediately on entering the café, and Scarlett's face showed signs that she recognised them but out of context. Hardwick was quick to put her mind at ease.

'Hello, Mrs Carr. We were just wondering if we might have a quick word regarding your husband again. We popped round to your house and your father said we might find you here.'

'Yes, of course,' she said, before turning to her friend. 'You don't mind, do you, Liz? We've got no secrets from each other, you see,' she said to Hardwick and Flint.

Hardwick somehow doubted this was entirely true. 'Ah, that's good. Because we wanted to ask you specifically about Kevin McGready.'

Scarlett's face changed in an instant. 'On second thoughts, Liz, could I catch up with you a bit later? It's a bit tight for space in here and I think this might take a while.'

The friend gone, Hardwick and Flint sat down on the small wooden chairs at the small wooden table in the small wooden café (no doubt the owners and clientele would christen it 'cosy' or 'chic').

A young man in a striped shirt and apron glided over to

their table and took their order before gliding back off to prepare it for them.

Scarlett leaned forward and whispered in anxious tones. 'Who have you been speaking to?'

Before Ellis could even think of saying the word 'Facebook', Hardwick had begun. 'If you'll forgive us, Mrs Carr, it's our job to speak to people. Could you tell us a little about your connection with Mr McGready?'

'He's a friend.'

'A close friend?' Ellis asked.

'Yes, in many ways. Why? What's this got to do with Elliot's death?'

'That's what we're trying to ascertain, Mrs Carr,' Hardwick replied. 'Let me get straight to the point. Were you having an affair with Kevin McGready?' Hardwick watched Scarlett's eyes carefully for any flicker or sign which might tell him more.

'Why would you ask a thing like that?' Scarlett asked calmly, not giving anything away.

Whilst Hardwick was still analysing this, Ellis seized the moment. 'Or perhaps you could tell us what "you sure E hasn't cottoned on" and "he doesn't have the intelligence — we're safe" means?'

Hardwick opened and closed his mouth like a freshly-caught fish gasping at the air as Scarlett responded.

'Where did you get that from?'

Don't say Facebook, Hardwick willed silently. *Don't say Facebook.*

'Could you tell us what it means?' Ellis insisted calmly. Hardwick was quietly impressed.

Scarlett stayed silent for a moment, her eyes blinking wildly as she considered what she should say.

'Well, what's the point? You know anyway, don't you?' she replied, turning it back on them again.

'Why don't you tell us what we know?' Ellis said. 'We can only suspect things until we know the truth. So why don't you tell us? Just so we know for sure.'

'Okay, why don't you tell me what you *suspect*?' she replied.

'We suspect that you and Kevin McGready were having an affair behind your husband's back, Mrs Carr,' Hardwick said. 'And that his finding out about it might have contributed to his mental state and reasons for committing suicide. In other words, your actions might have culminated, ultimately, in your husband's death.'

'What are you trying to say?' Scarlett asked, having cottoned on to the subtext immediately. 'That I made him do it?'

'That's a rather peculiar conclusion to jump to, isn't it?' Hardwick replied.

'Is it? What do you mean? Are you trying to say you think it might not have been suicide? That *I* might have killed my husband?'

'Somebody might have done, yes,' Ellis said, sensing that Hardwick's response might be less than diplomatic. 'We have to pursue all lines of enquiry, madam.' Ellis noted Hardwick glaring at him with a look of thunder.

'But the other officers we spoke to said there was no question of foul play. The coroner seems to have agreed so far.'

'As he said, we need to investigate all possibilities,' Hardwick said. 'Now, I think you need to tell us the whole truth about your relationship with Mr McGready, don't you?'

Over the course of the next hour, Scarlett spoke remarkably openly and honestly about her relationships with both her husband and her lover. Hardwick knew she was being remarkably open and honest because his own research had already told him most of the details, but he had wanted to see how much Scarlett would attempt to hide.

She told them that she and Elliot had married five years ago, quite soon after meeting. She said she knew straight away that he was the one for her, although Hardwick suspected that his large salary might have contributed to her sudden falling in love. She went on to explain that as the years had gone on, she realised she had made the decision too quickly and that she should have taken the time to get to know Elliot better.

Not that he was a bad man, she explained; they were just 'somewhat incompatible' as she put it. Hardwick assumed this meant that he was a level-headed man who'd worked hard to get a good job and earn a good salary and his wife had failed to do either, but instead rather enjoyed being on the receiving and spending end of said salary.

She explained that she had met Kevin McGready in a wine bar one night when out with friends. She'd thrown her friends off the scent by saying he was an old school friend and they quickly forgot all about it. Over the next few days and weeks they'd chatted on Facebook and by text and had begun to meet up regularly whilst Elliot was at work, the relationship quickly becoming serious.

'And do you think Elliot had found out about your relationship with Kevin?' Ellis asked as he took a sip of his third mug of coffee.

'No, I don't. He would've said something,' Scarlett replied.

'But you've already said that he was quite a private person and that he kept his feelings bottled up. Is there any chance he could've kept this bottled up?'

'Well, there's always a chance,' she said. 'But even though he kept his feelings to himself, he had principles. As far as he was concerned, cheating was wrong. Completely wrong. And it is as far as I'm concerned too, but this was different.' Scarlett noticed Hardwick's raised eyebrow and tried to elaborate. 'It's very difficult to explain until you're in that situation. Have you never loved two people at the same time?'

Hardwick explained that he hadn't.

'Well with me and Kevin it was different. I can't explain it, but it was. As for Elliot finding out, though, I know for a fact that he would've said something had he found out.'

'Would he say something straight away, though?' Ellis

asked. 'Or would he have perhaps waited to find the right moment? Is it possible that bottling it all up, even for a little while, could've put him in the position where he was forced over the edge? Perhaps the argument that night and the alcohol might have contributed.'

'I don't know,' she replied. 'It's possible. I just don't know what to think any more.'

14

The short train journey back to South Heath was beset by the usual delays: late trains, signal failures, technical issues on the line. The excuses came thick and fast, but regular users of the line were more than used to it and stopped taking any notice after a while.

'So what did you make of that, then, Kempston?' Ellis asked, already knowing the answer but asking the question anyway. 'Bit suspicious that she jumped to the conclusion that not only had Elliot been murdered, but that she was our main suspect too. Not sure that's the natural response.'

'If you mean do I think she killed her husband, Ellis, I don't know. I doubt it. Her only motive seems to be that she'd have him out of the way to shack up with her new lover. I don't see her resorting to murder, though. No, she'd do much better out of a divorce. Financially, anyway. And money seems to be at the forefront of her mind most of the time.'

'True. Plus if her husband committed suicide she'd not get a penny anyway. Most life insurance companies don't pay out in the event of suicide,' Ellis offered.

'Indeed. Which leaves two possibilities in my mind. Firstly, that Elliot Carr committed suicide knowing that Scarlett was going to leave him. He couldn't bear to live without her knowing she was with another man, knew divorce would leave her living off his earnings at the same time and also knew that by committing suicide he wouldn't have to live in that situation and that she wouldn't get a penny of his. Quite a nice little plan, if you think about it. Secondly, did you notice how Scarlett was the one who brought up the possibility of her husband being murdered? That could mean that she is well aware she'd not get a penny if his death was considered to be suicide so is trying to ensure a different outcome in order to profit financially. Or, even more sinister, that she was responsible for his death for the same reasons.'

'But why would she make it look like suicide? If it looked like an accident, or even a murder but leaving no possibility of it being her, she'd be home and dry without the added complication of a suicide outcome. Even a hired hitman would've been a better idea.'

'Very true, Ellis. Very true. But that all depends on how much thought was put into it, doesn't it? And you're also assuming that Scarlett Carr had the nouse to actually put a plan together and go through with it. Perhaps she did. Perhaps that plan went wrong. Perhaps this isn't what was meant to happen. Either way, it's all rather odd, isn't it?'

Ellis shuffled his feet, which he had a habit of doing when he was thinking. 'Depends if she had some help, really. Say this Kevin McGready bloke is a bit of a wrong'un, knows a few dodgy people. Do you reckon he could've had something to do with it?'

'Until we speak to him, Ellis, I don't know. What I do know, though, is that he's certainly on the list of suspects.'

15

Scarlett's hands shook with adrenaline as she dialled the number on her phone and waited for Kevin to answer. It only took three rings, but to Scarlett it felt like an age.

Before he could even answer, Scarlett jumped straight in. 'Kevin, I've just had those detectives on my back again. They found me in town somehow. Listen, they know about us. About me and you.'

'What? How? What did you tell them?' came the reply.

'I didn't tell them anything. Well, not anything serious. They knew about us seeing each other. They found Facebook messages. I had to admit to that much because they had the messages.'

'Did you tell them any more?'

'No! I'm not stupid, Kevin. I just told them the bare basics.'

'Good. Because the last thing we need is to give them a

bit of string to run with. If they find out about... Well, you know.'

'Yes, I know. Like I said, I'm not stupid. Listen, I think they've got everything they wanted from me.'

Scarlett could hear Kevin sighing at the other end of the phone. 'They'll find out eventually, you know, Scarlett.'

'No they won't. No-one ever has to know.'

16

Kimberly Gray pulled up the handbrake on her Vauxhall Astra as the car came to a stop on the gravel outside the Manor Hotel.

'I did give you your room key back, didn't I?' her friend Rhiannon asked from the front passenger seat.

'Yeah, it's in my handbag,' Kimberly replied, unbuckling her seatbelt and getting out of the car. She glanced through the rear passenger window into the back seat. 'Looks like we might need to wake Charlotte up.' She banged her fist on the window of the car, chuckling as her friend was startled back to consciousness. 'Come on, I need a bloody drink. It's all right for you sleeping it off already, but the designated driver's thirsty.'

'She should probably go straight to bed,' Rhiannon said as she opened the door to let Charlotte out of the car.

'Nope, not doing that,' Charlotte said, slurring slightly. 'Just tired, that's all. Let's go to the bar for a bit.'

Kimberly and Rhiannon exchanged glances, then Kimberly locked the car and followed the other two into the hotel.

Once they were at the bar, Kimberly took great joy in catching up with her friends' levels of alcohol consumption, having not been able to drink at the gig thanks to having been the driver. The girls had mulled over whether or not to order a taxi, but the cost would have been extortionate. Besides which, everyone at the gig would be ordering taxis as there was nothing within walking distance of Everidge Farm. As Kimberly's car was the one they'd travelled to South Heath in, and as she was the only one of the three with a driving licence, she'd drawn the short straw. She was doing her best to catch up now, though.

Having seen how long it took the woman behind the bar to get the ice machine working for Rhiannon's gin and tonic, Kimberly decided to stick to white wine. Her parents tended to drink red at home, but she wasn't keen. A nice sweet white was more her thing.

Charlotte had gone from a state of semi-consciousness to pure hyperactivity as she recalled the events of the gig that evening. Kimberly could feel herself loosening up as the alcohol mixed with the adrenaline in her bloodstream while they discussed the gig.

'Good night, was it?' the woman behind the bar asked. She seemed older than most hotel bar people. More like a chambermaid than a barmaid. Judging by her ability to operate the ice machine and her constant hunting around for glasses, Kimberly supposed that she wasn't the usual bar person.

'Yeah, we went to see Alex Alvarez at Everidge Farm,' Rhiannon said.

'Bloody brilliant, it was. We were about thirty feet away from him at one point,' Kimberly added. 'And I *swear* he looked at me at one point.'

'He looks at everyone. That's his thing. He makes his fans feel special,' Rhiannon said.

'Is he the Mexican chap?' the woman behind the bar asked. 'The one who's always on TV with all the girls screaming after him?'

'That's him,' Kimberly said. 'He's a God. A sex god!' The other girls laughed. The woman behind the bar smiled uneasily and raised her eyebrows.

Old people never quite got it. Sad thing is, she'd probably been the same when she was her age, Kimberly thought. No doubt she'd thought the same about Rolf Harris or Gary Glitter or whichever sad old man had been big at the time. She knew that Alex Alvarez wouldn't go the same way, though. Alex Alvarez, she knew, was flawless.

For the next couple of hours, whenever the old woman was at the bar, Kimberly would make a point of talking about the gig and how much of an icon Alex Alvarez was. She could see her getting more and more annoyed as the evening went on but she didn't once say a word. In a way, Kimberly admired her. She knew she wouldn't have that level of patience if people were trying to wind her up.

Charlotte, in the end, had only lasted another forty minutes or so after they arrived back before having to head up to bed, finally admitting that she should have gone straight up after they'd got back from the gig. She hadn't seemed completely drunk to Kimberly, but then again Charlotte didn't have a particularly high tolerance for alcohol.

'Christ, it's two o'clock,' Kimberly said as she finished off yet another glass of white wine. She wasn't sure if she was more worried about the fact that she'd have to drive in a few hours or that she could've saved a fair bit of money by getting whole bottles instead of buying it by the glass.

'And?' Rhiannon replied, clearly more than happy to stay here much longer and sleep it off in the car on the way home tomorrow.

'And I've got to drive home in the morning. I'll probably still be over the limit.'

'Nah, you'll be fine. You're sleeping in between anyway,' Rhiannon said, waving her hand dismissively.

'It doesn't work like that. I've only just got my licence and I don't want to lose it,' Kimberly replied.

'You're always so bloody boring,' Rhiannon said, putting her finger in the air to try and attract the attention of the woman behind the bar in order to ask for another drink.

'Look, I'm going to bed anyway,' Kimberly said. 'I'm not bothered whether you stay or not but I've had enough now.'

'Fine. Do as you want,' Rhiannon replied, counting out the change for her order.

SATURDAY 21ST MARCH

17

Hardwick had sent Ellis off to speak to Kevin McGready. In the meantime, he'd set his mind to locating Owen Bartlett, the member of staff who'd been working behind the bar at the Manor Hotel on the night Elliot Carr died, and who had spent most of the evening chatting with him. The same Owen Bartlett who'd then handed in his resignation and disappeared later that evening.

Ellis puffed out his chest as he pressed the buzzer next to the label reading Flat 5. Until now, Hardwick had rarely let him conduct his own interviews or speak to suspects on his own during an investigation. It was difficult enough, granted, to do so without arousing the suspicion of the local constabulary but Ellis was of the opinion that they could work far more efficiently by splitting up. Fortunately for him, Hardwick had agreed on this occasion.

'Yep?' came the voice through the speaker. Sharp and

to the point, much like Ellis had expected Kevin McGready to be.

'Mr McGready? Hello, my name's Ellis Flint. I'd just like to have a quick word with you about a police investigation.'

No response. Ellis had panicked himself slightly, but he ran back over his words in his mind. Nope, he hadn't actually said he was a police officer. The intercom made a clicking sound and the door buzzed to let him know it was unlocked. He unlocked the door, closed it behind him and made his way up the stairwell to Flat 5.

When he got there, the door to the flat was already open and a tall, muscular man in a tight white t-shirt was waiting for him.

'Kevin McGready?' Ellis said, offering his hand. The man hesitated for a moment before shaking it.

'Must admit we don't get many cops coming round here. They don't tend to get a great reception from the locals.'

'Well, I'm not here on any sort of official business,' Ellis said, truthfully. 'I just wondered if I might ask you a couple of questions, just to clarify a few things.'

'About what?' Kevin McGready said, furrowing his brow. 'I've kept my nose clean.'

'Oh yes, we know,' Ellis replied as the man ushered him through into the small living room. 'It's just that it concerns somebody you know and we need to find out as much about their relationships and connections as we can.'

'I ain't no grass if that's what you're saying. If you're hoping I'll drop someone in it, you should think again.'

'No, no, that's not what I meant at all,' Ellis said, by now getting flustered. 'What I meant was... Well, it's about Scarlett Carr.'

McGready's jaw tightened and he lifted his chin slightly before he spoke. 'What about her?'

'Would I be right in thinking that you were having a... romantic... relationship with her?'

'What's it got to do with you?'

'Oh, nothing. Well, potentially something. I don't know. It's about the death of her husband, you see.'

'I heard. Topped himself.'

'Yes. That's right. Well, possibly not. We don't know. That's what we're trying to work out,' Ellis said, trying desperately to dry his palms, which were by now sweating profusely, on his trouser legs. 'What I mean to say is, was Scarlett Carr planning to leave her husband for you?'

'Let me ask you something,' McGready said, taking a step towards Ellis. 'Did you ever meet Elliot Carr?'

'Well, no, I didn't,' Ellis replied.

'Right. In that case you won't know that he was a weasel, will you? A weak, pathetic little man who could barely make himself happy, let alone anyone else. Women like Scarlett, they don't want men like him. They want men who are stronger, command more authority. More power. Do you see what I mean, *officer*?' Kevin McGready was now mere inches from Ellis's face.

'Yes, yes, I think I do,' was all Ellis could say.

'So if she was planning to leave him for me, and I'm not saying she was, then I wouldn't be particularly surprised. She deserved better. Needed better. And yeah, if he'd found out then it doesn't surprise me at all that he's the sort of bloke who'd top himself.'

Ellis tried desperately to regain some ground and some control. 'Where were you on the night Elliot Carr died, Mr McGready?' he asked.

Kevin McGready stayed silent for a few moments before responding. 'As far as I'm aware, I don't need to answer questions like that unless I'm under arrest. Am I under arrest, *officer*?'

'Well, no...'

'No, I didn't think so. If you want to ask me any more personal questions, you can arrest me first. Is that clear, *officer*?'

'Yep. Yep. Perfectly clear,' Ellis said in a high-pitched voice, backing away from Kevin McGready and heading for the door. 'Very sorry to trouble you. Thank you for your time.'

18

Hardwick's feet clip-clopped across the parquet flooring as he went to answer the front door at the Old Rectory.

'Ah, Ellis. How did it go earlier?' he said, as he opened the door.

'Yep, fine.'

'Fine?' Hardwick asked.

'Yep. No problems.'

'What did he say?'

'Oh, well, not a lot,' Ellis replied. 'To be honest, he wasn't very talkative. Well, he was, but he wasn't. He wasn't very helpful. That's what I mean.'

Hardwick sighed and walked into his kitchen before sitting at the wooden table.

'What did you do, Ellis?'

'Nothing,' he replied, looking like a child who'd been dragged into the headmaster's office. 'I just asked him about his relationship with Scarlett and where he'd been on the night Elliot died.'

'And what did he say?'

'He said we'd have to arrest him to find out.'

'Brilliant. Just brilliant. So now our only way to find out any more from the mouth of Kevin McGready is if we can somehow convince DI Warner that Elliot Carr's death was suspicious and that McGready had something to do with it. Which will be very difficult to prove seeing as he probably won't speak to us again.'

'Sorry,' Ellis said.

'Let's just hope he didn't have anything to do with it, then, and we won't need to worry. Correction: *you* won't need to worry. Fortunately for you, we have other avenues we can pursue. While you've been out, I've been doing a bit of digging of my own. Not quite the same sort of digging as you, though. I've managed to find out where Owen Bartlett lives. Or, rather, where his mother lives. He'd been lodging with a family in South Heath while he was working at the Manor Hotel, but he came back from work on the night Elliot Carr died and said his mother was ill and that he had to go back home to Brighton to care for her. He caught an overnight train and was gone.'

'Brighton? Blimey. And do you know if it was true, about his mother?'

'I very much doubt it,' Hardwick said. 'Not unless she's made a miraculous recovery. I checked her Facebook profile and she's been surfing in Newquay, trekking over the South Downs and clubbing in Brighton. All within the past week.'

'You and Facebook. You'll get addicted,' Ellis said, only half joking.

'Unlikely, Ellis.'

'How old is his mother then? She sounds quite young and active.'

'Sixty-five. This is Brighton, after all, Ellis.'

Before Ellis could respond, Hardwick's phone rang. He walked into his living room and picked up the receiver. After a short, murmured conversation that Ellis couldn't hear, Hardwick came back into the kitchen.

'That was Doug from the Freemason's Arms, Ellis. He thought we might be interested to know that there's been another suicide at the Manor Hotel.'

19

Doug Lilley was not a man who let things get to him, which was just as well living in a place like Tollinghill. He chuckled slightly as he patted himself down with paper towels after the third barrel of beer had erupted over him in the cellar that day. It was a fairly regular occurrence and all part of being a pub landlord, but three in one day was pretty rare. Extreme changes in the weather were often to blame. Perhaps there was a storm on the way, he thought, or some sort of atmospheric change.

Back at the top of the stairs and behind the bar, he called out to the large man sat perched on his usual stool.

'The Spunky Monkey's back on, Sid. All ten pints of it, anyway. The rest of it's soaked into my shirt if you want it.'

'I'll pass thanks mate,' Sid replied. 'So what did your detective mate have to say for himself?'

'Not a lot,' Doug said. 'As per usual. He's not one to

talk unless he's got something to say, if you see what I mean.'

'Same for most of us, though, ain't it?' Sid replied.

'Speak for yourself. What I mean is that he's a thinker, isn't he? Likes to mull over things, work out what's gone on. He won't go spouting any theories until he's pretty sure.'

'Miserable bugger if you ask me.'

'Which I didn't. Nothing wrong with keeping yourself to yourself, is there? Perhaps you should take a leaf out of his book, Sid.'

'Charming, that is. There's plenty of other good pubs round here I could drink in, y'know.'

'No there isn't,' Doug replied.

'Fair point. Bit weird that there's been two deaths, though, ain't it?'

'Well yeah, that's why I called him. If there's something a bit funny going on, he'll get to the bottom of it. Not as if the local coppers are going to do much good. They only call him for help half the time anyway.'

'Wouldn't surprise me if he was bumping them off to give himself the work,' Sid said before taking a gulp of his pint.

'Do you ever have anything good to say about people, Sid? Besides, he doesn't get paid anything. He's "a man of independent means" as he puts it. So you can cut that rubbish out straight away. No, I reckon there's got to be something dodgy going on there. Something not quite right. Kempston'll get to the bottom of it, don't you worry.'

'Doubt that very much,' said the voice of Jez Cook, who'd managed to float into the pub unheard and plant himself at the end of the bar nearest the entrance. 'All seems a bit too clever for me.'

'Most things seem a bit too clever for you, Jez,' Doug said, heading down his end of the bar. 'That's why you've been inside three times.'

'Yeah, but it's what they ain't caught me for that's the real story, ain't it? What's good today?'

'It's all good. Serving crap doesn't tend to go down too well business-wise. But then again you'd know all about that.'

'I'll have you know my crap's got a very good reputation locally,' Jez replied.

'Well the police certainly know all about it, don't they? Bloody good job you're not able to shift any of it since the Black Horse shut down. Which reminds me. If you're even thinking of bringing anything like that in here you can get out now while I'm asking nicely.'

'Woah, relax,' Jez said, raising his hands in mock surrender. 'I'm just here for a pint, all right? Nothing like that.'

'Right. Well make it just the one and be on your way then,' Doug said.

'Blimey. Talk about things being bad for business,' Jez mumbled under his breath, having pointed to the beer he wanted.

'Three-twenty. And no, you can't stick it on the tab,' Doug said, jumping in before Jez could speak again.

'How's that for customer service?' he replied, fishing deep in his pockets for the right change. 'Anyway, what's been said about all this business down at the Manor then?'

'How do you mean?' Doug replied, taking the money from him and putting it in the till. As he did so, he noticed a man he didn't know sitting at the far end of the bar next to the cider pumps, his pint almost finished, looking intently at Jez.

'Well, I should imagine it's the talk of the town ain't it? Bit weird having two people top themselves in that short a time in the same place. And doing it the same way and all. And seeing as they didn't know each other...'

'What, so you're Columbo as well as Al Capone now are you?' Doug said, laughing.

'Nah, nothing like that. But it's weird, ain't it? I mean, both being hung by a dressing gown cord in the same room. Neither of them depressed or nothing. No reason to want to top themselves, like.'

'What, so you reckon we've got a serial killer on the loose now?' Sid chipped in.

'Wouldn't be the first time, would it?' Jez replied. 'And anyway, it's not a serial killer till you've got three victims. It's just a double murder.'

'The police don't seem to think so,' Doug said, mopping down the bar with a dishcloth.

'Not at the moment. But they will do. They've got to see it sooner or later, ain't they?'

'You think there'll be more deaths?' Doug asked.

'Wouldn't surprise me,' Jez said. 'Have to wait and see, won't we?'

At the other end of the bar by the cider pumps, Kevin McGready swallowed heavily as he finished the last dregs of his pint, stood up, pushed the stool back against the bar and left the Freemason's Arms.

SUNDAY 22ND MARCH

20

Although Hardwick was reluctant to allow Ellis to set off down to Brighton on his own after the less-than-successful episode with Kevin McGready, he also knew that time was not on their side. The revelation of a second suicide at the Manor Hotel had stirred a worrying and impending sense of doom within Hardwick. Although he had no details, he knew that it did not bode well.

It was only through sheer necessity, then, that Ellis Flint stepped aboard the direct train to Brighton, a two-hour journey which would see him snake through the centre of London and across Blackfriars Bridge before zipping through the Surrey and Sussex countryside and nestling quietly at the end of the railway in Brighton's impressive railway station.

The idea of walking long distances didn't fill Ellis with joy, his calves still aching from following a marching Hardwick to and from the Manor Hotel in South Heath.

However, he didn't much fancy shelling out for a city centre taxi and, by all accounts, the traffic he could see backed up outside the station meant that walking would probably be the quickest option anyway. Speak to Owen Bartlett, find out what went on and get to a nice local pub before heading back. That was the plan.

The pavements of Queen's Road, the main thorough-fare from the station to the seafront, were heaving as Ellis waddled down the hill past all manner of shops and office fronts. At the busy North Street junction, he headed east past the boutique shops and welcoming pubs before crossing the Steine Gardens and making his way up the hill into Kemp Town, the bohemian centre of Brighton.

Ellis was not a man who explored, but that was not to say that he didn't enjoy it. He was just quite happy knocking around Tollinghill and keeping his life as easy and carefree as possible. Which wasn't always the case since he'd met Kempston Hardwick. The closest he'd come to anything resembling the bustling bonhomie of Kemp Town was being dragged through Soho, twice, by Hard-wick in order to interview a stripper in a seedy 'gentle-men's' club three years earlier.

Yes, he was here on business, but he was alone and didn't have to concentrate on trying to keep up with Kemp-ston Hardwick, be it mentally or physically.

When he finally arrived at St George's Terrace, he located Owen Bartlett's mother's house and walked up the steps to the front door. A young man, probably in his early to mid twenties, Ellis assumed, opened the door.

'Oh. Hello,' Ellis said, having not expected the search to be quite this easy. 'I was expecting to see Mrs Bartlett. Is she in?' Ellis asked, for no reason at all other than to say something — anything — to give him some space to get his brain back on track.

'Uh, no, she's not. Why?'

'Are you Owen Bartlett?' Ellis asked, ignoring the man's question.

'Depends who's asking,' the man replied.

'I'm here about the death of a man at the Manor Hotel in South Heath, where you worked until very recently, Owen,' Ellis said, attempting to read some flicker of emotion from the man's eyes. What he saw, or thought he saw, was danger.

'Not here, okay?' came the reply. 'I'll talk, but meet me up the road at the Sidewinder in ten minutes.'

It struck Ellis as a little odd that Owen wouldn't want to discuss the matter at home, and his suspicion led him to get as far as the end of St George's Terrace before crouching behind a wheelie-bin as he waited for Owen Bartlett to leave the house and walk the short distance to the Sidewinder pub.

A few minutes later, Owen left the house, descended the steps and walked purposefully towards the end of the street. Once he'd passed the corner, Ellis gave him a few yards' head start before following him across the green outside some flats and onto Upper St James's Street, where he walked into the Sidewinder as planned.

Ellis walked in a few moments after Owen, and

explained he'd gone for a little walk to 'get his bearings' before coming to the pub. The pub was beautifully traditional, with a wooden floor, wooden tables and a very friendly atmosphere. Ellis was thankful that he hadn't been led into a rough estate pub in which he'd find it very difficult to interview Owen Bartlett, but rather felt very comfortable and secure, which inspired his direct line of questioning.

'I'll get straight to the point,' Ellis said, as they sat down at a round wooden table with their pints of beer. 'I'm told you resigned from your job and left quite suddenly on the night Elliot Carr died. Is that right?'

'Yeah. Yeah, it is,' Owen said.

'Can you tell me why?'

'Well why do you think?' he replied. Ellis opened his mouth to tell him exactly why he thought he'd upped and gone, but thought better of it. 'Look, I hadn't been happy there for a while, all right? And I've not been well, truth be told. Depression and that. So when that bloke topped himself I just couldn't take it any more. I had to get out.'

'Had there been problems at the hotel before?' Ellis asked.

'Nothing like that, no. I just mean in general. I mean, South Heath's not quite Brighton, is it?'

You can say that again, Ellis thought. 'You mean you were homesick?'

'Yeah, if you like. I'd been at the hotel for a while and it just wasn't going anywhere. I wasn't happy. I'd been thinking of leaving for a while but that was just the icing on the cake for me.'

'Who found Mr Carr's body?' Ellis asked, knowing that Owen would either choose to lie for some reason, in which case he'd know he was hiding something, or would tell the truth, in which case he'd see which way his eyes flickered in order to have a marker for Owen's truth tells. Hardwick had always pooh-poohed Ellis's insistence that this method would make it very easy to spot who was lying and who was telling the truth, having told him on a number of occasions that it was unreliable and likely to cloud their judgement. *Stick to the facts, Ellis,* Hardwick would always say. *Sod the facts,* Ellis thought. *There are no facts.*

'I only know what I've been told. Apparently it was Derren. Derren Robson,' Owen said. Ellis thought he saw a mere flicker of the eyes to the upper-left, but his answer came too quickly for him to be sure.

'And am I right in thinking that you had quite a long conversation with Mr Carr at the bar that night?'

'Yeah, I did. There weren't many people in and he was just sat there looking pretty miserable so I humoured him.'

'Humoured him?' Ellis asked.

'Yeah, you know what I mean. Just listened to him and chatted.'

'And what was he miserable about?' Ellis asked. 'Did he say?'

'Something about an argument with his wife. It was meant to be their anniversary but she'd said or done something which had upset him, so he came down to the bar for a couple of drinks instead.'

'Did he say what she had said or done to upset him?'

'I dunno,' Owen said, taking a sip of his beer. 'I don't really remember. You get a lot of sob stories working behind a bar. People feel they can come to you with their problems, you know? Kind of what made me sick of the job in a way. I mean, we've all got our own problems, ain't we? Don't need no more grief from total strangers.'

'What problems do you have, Owen?' Ellis asked, turning more good-cop-agony-aunt as the conversation progressed. 'Money issues? Girl troubles?'

Owen scoffed and shook his head at the suggestion. 'Let's just say no.'

Ellis's brain, as was the norm, took a little while to catch up. Unfortunately for him, his mouth got there first. 'What do you mean?'

'There's not much of a gay scene in South Heath, is there?' Owen asked, trying to nudge Ellis's train of thought.

'Well no, there isn't. There are a couple of very good gay friendly nightclubs in Shafford, so I hear, which... Ah. I see,' Ellis replied, suddenly realising what he was meant to have already realised. 'Sorry. I didn't mean to offend you.'

'You didn't offend me,' Owen said. 'Contrary to popular belief, gay people aren't actually offended by women.'

'So were there man troubles?' Ellis offered.

'Just the usual,' Owen said, offering no further information. 'Look, I know it was probably stupid to just disappear like that, but it's not as if it really mattered, is it? I mean, it's just a job. I know a bloke died and that, but they didn't exactly need me hanging around.'

'That's just the problem,' Ellis said, clasping his hands and leaning forward as he prepared to drop the bombshell. 'It might well look very bad that you disappeared so quickly.'

'What do you mean?' Owen asked.

'We believe that Elliot Carr may have been murdered.'

Ellis watched as Owen Bartlett's face turned an even whiter shade of pale.

21

As much as Hardwick liked the Manor Hotel and admired the beautiful stone building and the grounds in which it stood, he had hoped not to be back any time soon.

The event of a second suicide at the hotel had meant that there was now very little doubt in Hardwick's mind that foul play was involved. This was confirmed when he popped in to the Freemason's Arms on his way to South Heath to speak to Doug Lilley, the landlord, who'd called him with the news about the second suicide.

Doug was well connected, not just as the landlord of a thriving pub in the small market town of Tollinghill, but as a member of the local Rotary Club and various other organisations. For him to be one of the first to hear of any local developments was certainly not surprising.

He had explained to Hardwick exactly what he had heard: that the second suicide was that of a young woman from London who'd been staying at the Manor Hotel with some friends to attend a local pop concert. She'd recently turned eighteen and had also passed her driving test in the past couple of weeks, so the event was something of a double celebration for her. What piqued Hardwick's interest, though, was the manner in which she'd died.

As with Elliot Carr, she'd been found hanging from the exposed rafters in room thirteen, the room which had been used for storage at the hotel, with a dressing gown cord acting as a noose. Again, a chair seemed to have been used to get to the rafter and subsequently kicked away. The suicide seemed to be identical in every way to that of Elliot Carr.

What was most infuriating for Hardwick, though, was that the local police force seemed to be completely unwilling to treat it as anything other than a suicide. Hardwick knew that Detective Inspector Rob Warner was not one for wanting to get his hands dirty and he also knew that pen ink and paper cuts were his least favourite ways to do it. True enough, he had plenty of sympathy with the modern police officer regarding the mountain of paperwork they had to fill in just to get a cup of coffee from the vending machine, but DI Warner sometimes took his aversion to protocol to the extreme.

Even now as he walked up to the front door of the Manor Hotel, before he'd even set foot inside and spoken to the hotel staff about what they saw, Hardwick was convinced that something else was at work. It would be convincing DI Warner of that which would prove to be the hardest task, though.

On entering the hotel and being ushered through to the bar by the ever-present Mandy, Hardwick noticed that the ageing technophobe Barbara was once again working behind the bar. No longer fancying a coffee, he ordered himself a Campari and orange.

'Ice?' Barbara asked, already heading to the ice machine before she'd had a response.

'Please.'

'That's if I can get this thing working. Don't know why they can't just have the ice in a bucket any more. Health and safety, I suppose. Instead I've got to push the glass against there, twist that and tug this. And with these arthritic hands, too. Can barely tie my own shoelaces with these things, never mind operate the Starship Enterprise here.'

Ten minutes later, after having watched Barabara wrestle with the ice machine, Hardwick had his drink.

'Starting to becoming a regular occurrence, seeing you in here,' Barbara said as she handed over the marbling liquid. The sharp, bitter aroma hit Hardwick's nostrils, making him salivate instantly.

'Yes, unfortunately so. I hear that there's been another suicide,' he said, in the manner of passing conversation.

'Oh, yes. Terrible thing. Only a young girl, too. Dreadful shame.'

'Indeed,' Hardwick replied, taking a sip of his drink as he handed over a handful of coins. 'Do you know what happened?'

'Well, yes. It was one of the poor maids who found her,

God bless her soul,' Barbara said, making the sign of the cross. 'The girl had been staying here overnight to go to a concert at Everidge Farm. Alex Alvarez, I think it was.' Alex Alvarez was a huge global pop star, the winner of America's foremost TV talent show, bringing a bizarre brand of Mexican-influenced rap to the masses.

Everidge Farm, colloquially known as "Evvers" amongst those who know those sorts of things, was a large area of farmland on which a permanent music stage had been erected, and was now home to large pop concerts and the like. Needless to say, Everidge Farm was no longer actually a working farm, making its more recent sobriquet far more fitting. It was also infinitely more marketable, for which its PR company was eternally grateful. *Come and see a concert at Everidge Farm* didn't quite have the same ring to it as *Thank 'eavens for Evvers*, and *Wherever, Whenever, Our Evvers* as twee but nonetheless successful marketing tag lines.

'This concert was last night, was it?' Hardwick asked, having already done his research but not wanting to seem too keen.

'Yes, it was. She was here with some friends — another two, I think. Yes, that's right. They had two rooms. Two of them were sharing one room and she was in the other. They came back after the concert and were at the bar until about two o'clock in the morning.'

'Is it open that late?' Hardwick asked.

'Until half past, yes. Bit daft of them really, as they had to drive back to London in the morning. Not very sensible for a new driver to risk something like that. I presumed they were getting the train back, else I would've suggested they didn't drink any more. Apparently Kimberly — that's the one who died — had only passed her test recently so it was a bit of a road trip for her.'

'Ah, I see. Perhaps it wouldn't be quite so easy on the train from their part of London?' Hardwick suggested, hoping to tease some further information out of Barbara, who seemed only too happy to talk.

'Greenford, they said, so yes. Straight round the M25 and up the M1. Would take forever on the train.'

'Oh, you spoke to them then?' Hardwick asked.

'Oh yes, absolutely. I was working behind the bar again. Been difficult since Owen left. I think because I live-in it's just easier for them to ask me to do things. Seeing as I'm always around anyway.'

'So did you get any idea as to why this Kimberly girl might want to kill herself?' Hardwick asked, trying to steer the conversation back onto topic.

'No, not really. I mean, she was quite emotional about it all when she got back. Saying how much she idolised this Alvarez chap. Can you imagine? But then again, you never know what goes on behind people's eyes, do you?'

'Very true,' Hardwick replied, before thanking Barbara for her time, draining his drink and heading for the exit. As far as he was concerned, Detective Inspector Rob Warner had some explaining to do.

As he passed the reception desk, Hardwick called over to the ever-present Mandy. 'Barbara said could I ask you to pop over to the lounge and help her with something on the bar. Something about an ice machine.'

'Ah!' Mandy replied, instantly diligent and assiduous. 'I'll just go and see what's the matter.'

As he heard Mandy's footsteps fading into the distance, Hardwick swung around in the porch, skipped back to the reception desk and glanced at the guest book, committing Kimberly's address to memory.

22

Detective Inspector Rob Warner was never happy at having to work on a Sunday, and particularly not on a Sunday afternoon. He had hoped that by now he would be sat at home with his feet up in front of the TV, watching the day's football results as they rolled in. No such luck.

Even a simple cut-and-dried suicide required a mountain of paperwork, as was the norm in modern-day policing. Warner often hankered after the days when he'd first joined the force, when coppers could be coppers. Sure, those days were filled with corruption, wrongful arrests and police brutality and crime rates had fallen drastically since then, with public safety increasing and corruption charges at an all-time low, but that wasn't the point. Warner liked things to be done in the old-fashioned way. It had worked for him just fine, thank you very much.

His afternoon was made slightly less bearable by the appearance of Kempston Hardwick at his office door.

Through numerous attempts at moving towards privatising the police service, successive governments had sought to introduce new 'initiatives', as they'd been marketed, in order to produce a more 'cohesive' and 'structured' approach to policing. The upshot of this is that they'd been encouraged to use more external assistance. Unfortunately for Warner, Kempston Hardwick counted as external assistance. Although he wasn't a qualified forensic scientist, distinguished psychological profiler or, hell, even a 'handwriting expert' with a certificate printed off the internet, Hardwick did have a knack of managing to solve crimes.

Hardwick's knocking at the door was forceful, indicative of him having a bee in his bonnet. Well, Hardwick always had a bee in his bonnet about something, but it wasn't usually a reason for him to be rapping at Warner's office door on a Sunday afternoon. No, Warner knew exactly why he was here. Kimberly Gray was practically still warm but he had no doubt that Hardwick had not only already heard about her death but had already formulated all sorts of wild theories about what had caused it. The fact that it was a clear suicide wouldn't deter him in the slightest.

Warner opened the door. 'Hardwick, how wond—'

I think we need to have a chat, Detective Inspector Warner,' Hardwick said, walking past Warner and his outstretched hand and sitting in the chair next to Warner's desk. 'Kimberly Gray,' he said, waiting for Warner to speak.

'What about her? It was a suicide, no doubt about it.'

'Has the pathologist confirmed yet?' Hardwick asked.

'No, of course not. She's barely been dead a few hours.'

'Well there you go then,' Hardwick said, as if this proved some sort of point.

'And before you say it: no, I don't think there is anything to link the suicides of Kimberly Gray and Elliot Carr.'

'Really? So the fact that they both died in the same room of the same hotel, using the same method of suicide and even the same way of doing it — with a dressing gown cord — and within a week of each other, doesn't seem in the slightest bit odd to you?'

'If those details had been kept back, perhaps. But the fact is that Elliot Carr's suicide made the local newspapers and even a couple of nationals. Slow news day, but what can you do? All of those details were publicly available. What's to say Kimberly Gray didn't read a report of Elliot Carr's suicide and plan to kill herself in the same way?'

'Why on earth would she do that?' Hardwick asked.

'Because people do. Copycat suicides. Just like copycat killers. There's a big market in it, unfortunately. There are literally hundreds of cases where people have committed crimes or murders based on others. And as for copycat suicides, they're more common than you'd think. Look at the Bridgend suicides.'

Between 2007 and 2012, there were seventy-nine known suicides in the Bridgend area of South Wales — an extraordinarily high number, considering the average before this period was around three to five a year. All involved young people, and in the first two years all but one death was due to hanging. The media dubbed it a 'cult suicide' phenomenon and were eventually asked to stop covering the suicides for fear of compelling more young people to take their own lives.

'That was on an enormous scale, Detective Inspector. You know that. Here, we're talking about just two suicides. Hardly a cult effect.'

'The Bridgend suicides had to start somewhere, Hardwick,' Warner said. 'Don't you worry, we're taking this very seriously. Anyone taking their own life is a tragedy, no doubt about it, and if there's any chance of these suicides being connected we'll ensure as best we can that we put a stop to it before any more lives are lost. But bear in mind that that's what they are. Suicides. We are not entertaining the idea that a third party was in any way involved.'

'And why not?' Hardwick asked. 'Surely you need to eliminate all possibilities instead of just defaulting to what happens to look most likely at the time? Most likely does not mean certain, Detective Inspector.'

Warner leaned forward on his chair and steepled his hands on his desk.

'Listen, Hardwick. If I had to treat every suicide or death as a murder investigation, it just wouldn't be possible. We have to use our knowledge and *experience*,' Warner said, emphasising the word, 'to uncover the facts and provide a satisfactory conclusion.'

'Satisfactory to whom?' Hardwick asked. He could see

he wasn't going to get anywhere and that Warner was not budging, so he had now decided to resort to making the man feel as idiotic as Hardwick felt he was.

'To everybody involved.'

'So not to the families of the deceased, then? Because I'm pretty sure that if there was even the slightest chance of someone else having been responsible for their loved ones' deaths, they'd want to know.'

'But there isn't the slightest chance, Hardwick. You have to accept that.'

'Do I? Isn't there? Can you honestly say, with one hundred percent certainty, Detective Inspector, that there is absolutely no chance whatsoever that you might just be missing something, however small or seemingly insignificant, which could possibly show otherwise?'

Hardwick could see Warner's jaw flexing as the Detective Inspector ground his teeth. 'Listen to me. You never know what's going on under the surface. People who should know better can't see that sometimes what's behind closed doors...' Warner trailed off as his voice began to crack. He took a moment before speaking again. 'The people who are left are the ones who feel guilty. They feel they should've known, seen it coming, done something. Trust me, it would almost be better if it were murder because then at least the people who were left would know it wasn't their fault.' He swallowed hard. 'But that's not the case here, Hardwick.' Hardwick watched with interest as Warner took a long blink and a deep breath. 'I think you should leave now.'

23

Ellis's train trundled in to South Heath station, the brakes squealing and hissing as the carriages came to a halt and the doors slid open. Cabs weren't cheap around here, but he'd be buggered if he was walking back to Tollinghill after all that traipsing around Brighton.

Granted, he didn't need to have covered the mileage that he did, but he'd found out from Googling on the way down that there were a number of good pubs and eateries in Brighton, and it would've been rude not to have tried a few of them. The day had seemed to be going well and the flowing beers had not tipped him over from tipsy into full-blown drunk thanks to the enormous meal he'd eaten at the American diner down on the sea front. His 'one last pint' at the Evening Star, near Brighton Station, had been his downfall. It wasn't his fault. He didn't have his glasses on at the time and couldn't see that it was an 11.5% Norwegian stout. Heigh-ho. Let the taxi take the strain.

He slid his backside ungracefully into the seat of the taxi and asked the driver to drop him at the Old Rectory in Tollinghill. It would be best that he didn't arrive home to Mrs F in this state. A few black coffees first would be a far better idea.

When Ellis got to Hardwick's house, he noticed that the front door was slightly ajar. This wasn't a particularly odd sight, as Hardwick often left his door slightly ajar when he didn't want to be disturbed by having to get up to answer the doorbell or, more frequently, when he couldn't be bothered to do so.

Ellis pushed the door open, stepped inside and closed it behind him before clip-clopping through into the kitchen, where he found Hardwick sat at the table, arms folded across his chest.

'Ah. You spoke to DI Warner, then?' Ellis asked, in his own observant way. Hardwick didn't reply. 'What did he say?' Ellis continued.

'What do you think he said, Ellis?' Hardwick said in a terse, tired voice.

'That despite the suicides of Elliot Carr and Kimberly Gray being almost identical and happening in the same room a week apart, he couldn't see a link.'

'Yes. Well no,' Hardwick said. 'He said he could see the link but explained it away by saying it must've been some sort of copycat suicide.'

'Like the Bridgend ones?' Ellis asked.

'Don't you start.'

'Seriously, though, he might have a point. How do we know it's not a copycat suicide?'

'I just know, Ellis, all right?' Hardwick replied, before petulantly thrusting his tongue into the inside of his cheek.

'I just mean... Well, like you always say, it's best to consider all of the possibilities before coming to a conclusion, right?' Again, Hardwick didn't reply. 'Mind if I make myself a coffee?' Ellis asked.

'Help yourself,' came the terse reply.

'Want one?'

'No.'

Ellis busied himself with making the coffee, taking a little longer than he was usually accustomed to. He was quite sure that at any moment Hardwick would have to say something. Hardwick, though, was a man who was more than happy to sit in silence if there was nothing to say. Eventually, as Ellis spooned the fifth sugar into his mug, he broke the silence.

'Look, Kempston, you've obviously got a feeling about this. I think the copycat suicide thing is worth looking into and I can see that you don't. So why don't I look into it? If it's a waste of my time then that's no problem. In the meantime, you can start to look at motives and stuff and follow the theory that they were murdered. Yeah?'

Hardwick sat in silence and nodded.

'Don't be upset, Kempston. You know what Warner's like. He'll do anything to get out of filling in another form. You stick to your guns. I'll keep him happy by looking at copycat suicides and stuff. Don't worry about it.'

For the first time since Ellis had arrived, Hardwick looked at him.

'You're a good man, Ellis,' he said.

MONDAY 23RD MARCH

24

The thoughts and possibilities rattled around Hardwick's head as he sat in his armchair with his eyes closed, trying to piece together the jigsaw of the deaths of Elliot Carr and Kimberly Gray without so much as the picture on the front of the box.

There seemed to be no link between the two apart from the manner in which they'd apparently killed themselves. Hardwick wasn't quite sure that they *had* killed themselves, though. He'd spent enough time catching murderers now to know when a death had been caused by someone else. His main problem was that he couldn't explain why he felt this way. Sure, there were inconsistencies with the suicide theory but that wouldn't be enough to convince DI Warner or anyone else that a third party was responsible for the deaths of Elliot Carr and Kimberly Gray.

His only real ally seemed to be Ellis. Unfortunately,

Ellis wasn't quite as preoccupied with the theory of murder as he was with the notion that some sort of supernatural, paranormal force was at play and somehow responsible for the deaths. This wasn't a theory that Hardwick was particularly keen to entertain.

But if it was murder, who murdered them? From what he'd been told, Kimberly Gray had no real enemies to speak of, there was no sign of any sexual interference and no-one had any motive to kill her. Elliot Carr's wife, Scarlett, did have a motive in that she had a secret lover who she'd planned to leave Elliot for, plus she was at the scene of the crime. If there was a crime. Hardwick was sure there was. But if there was only one killer, that would mean Scarlett had killed Kimberly Gray, too. Why? The only other theory was that Kimberly Gray's death was not a copycat suicide, but a copycat murder. Again, the same problem arose: no-one wanted Kimberly Gray dead.

Something was missing. Some piece of the puzzle hadn't yet been found and that frustrated Hardwick, knowing that he couldn't get to the bottom of what had happened no matter how hard he tried, because a vital piece of information was still missing.

His frustration was cut short by the ringing of his doorbell. He made his way to the front door of the Old Rectory and opened it to find Detective Inspector Rob Warner stood on his doorstep with a manila folder under his arm.

'Morning. Can I come in?' Warner asked as he came in anyway.

'Yes, of course, why not?' Hardwick replied over his

shoulder. 'Why don't you make your way through to the living room?' he added as Warner rounded the corner into the living room.

By the time Hardwick had sat down in his armchair, Warner had already opened the manilla folder and had begun leafing through what looked to be a stack of bank statements.

'These are the financial records we obtained regarding Elliot and Scarlett Carr,' Warner said, getting straight to the point. 'Here, a credit card with £36,340 outstanding. That was originally a balance transfer of just under forty grand, paying off three other credit cards, here,' he said, showing Hardwick another three sets of statements. 'Interestingly, they're all cards in Scarlett's sole name. The new card which consolidated them all was in their joint names.'

'Presumably Elliot would've known about that, then, in order to give authorisation for it to have been set up,' Hardwick said. 'Besides, Scarlett wouldn't have needed to share the debt as such, as they were married so it would've been joint debt anyway, wouldn't it?'

'That all depends. It can get tricky and messy. There were also finance agreements against two cars: the 3-series Beamer and a Range Rover Evoque. The Evoque was in for repairs, apparently.'

'Blimey. They don't have much luck on the car front, then.'

'Less a case of mechanical failure on the Evoque and more the fact that Scarlett had reversed it into a lamppost, apparently,' Warner said, chuckling. 'Anyway, the point is there's nearly forty grand still owing on the BMW's finance and just under thirty on the Evoque. Plus the house had been mortgaged to the hilt.'

'Christ,' Hardwick said. 'How did they manage to get all that credit?'

'Well, Elliot had a decent job,' Warner said. 'Once they'd got that house, finance companies and banks would throw credit at them. They know a house in Bellingham is worth its weight in gold.'

'I presume you're going to tell me they were struggling to keep up with paying it back,' Hardwick said.

'Oh yes,' Warner replied. 'Even with a job like Elliot's, that's just a stupid amount of credit. All interest bearing, too. He'd tried to minimise the growth of it by shifting the cards across to a lower rate, which shows he was wise to it, if not worried about it. We know from his chats at the bar and our own experience of Scarlett Carr that we can quite safely say she would've wanted those cars, that house and probably 90% of the items bought with the credit cards.'

'So you're suggesting that Elliot Carr killed himself to escape the debt?' Hardwick asked, skeptically.

'It's looking likely. And even to possibly punish Scarlett. It was her debt after all, and he knew that if he topped himself the life insurance wouldn't pay out, so she'd be lumbered with it all on her own. God forbid, she'd even have to get a job.'

'Interestingly enough, I did my own research and found out that she'd been having a bit of a dalliance with a local chap called Kevin McGready,' Hardwick said.

'There you go, then. Combine the debt problem and the secret boyfriend and you've got a pretty good reason to want to top yourself, haven't you?' Warner said.

'I can see exactly what you're saying, but I'm still not sure I'm convinced,' Hardwick said. 'It sounds like a rather good motive for murder to me. And anyway, your suicide theory still doesn't explain Kimberly Gray's death.'

'It doesn't need to. They were separate incidents with nothing linking them,' Warner said. Hardwick didn't bother to reply and instead chose to roll his eyes. There was no point in going over old ground again. Warner wouldn't be swayed.

'What did the forensics people say about the scene?' Hardwick finally asked, breaking the silence. 'About the chair positioning, I mean. Was it commensurate with the victims having kicked them away?'

'I think you mean the deceased, Hardwick. Victims require murderers. And to answer your question, it's an open verdict on that. Yes, it's entirely possible that Elliot Carr and Kimberly Gray kicked the chairs away. If you're asking me could someone else have done so, then yes, of course, if they were stood facing the same way. That can never be definitely ruled out, but take it from me: it's as positive as it can be that there was no foul play involved.'

'I see,' Hardwick said, mostly for the sake of having to say something.

'Now, you'll understand that everything I've told you is confidential, of course. And purely to put your mind at rest that nothing strange has been going on. No murders, no conspiracies, nothing. The motives and reasons for Elliot Carr killing himself are clear. So I want you to drop this bee in your bonnet. Do you understand?' Warner asked.

Hardwick chose his words very carefully. 'Yes, I understand what you want.'

Warner had been gone less than two minutes when there was an odd bang at the front door. Hardwick got up and quickly walked into the hall, flinging the door open with force. There was no-one there. As he was about to close the door again, he noticed a sheet of folded paper nailed to it. Leaving the nail in place, he tore the sheet of paper from it, unfolded it and read.

STOP STICKING YOUR NOSE WHERE ITS NOT WANTED. KEEP OUT OF ARE LIVES AND BUTT OUT UNLESS YOU WANT TO BE NEXT. YOUVE BEEN WARNED.

More offended by the dreadful spelling than the death threat, Hardwick furrowed his brow and glanced quickly around the front garden, knowing full well that the perpetrator would be long gone by now. He went back inside, closing and locking the door behind him.

25

As much as Ellis liked a drink, he was not a big fan of hang-overs. Tiredness he could deal with, but hangovers were not something he could abide. Fuelled with black coffee and half a bag of sugar, then, he booted up his laptop and decided to do some research on copycat suicides.

His first port of call was to do some more research into the Bridgend suicide phenomenon. Like most people in the UK, he had been well aware of the basics of the case as it had been widely reported in the media, but had since fizzled out and become a rather blurred memory. On the other hand, most of Ellis Flint's memories were rather blurred.

He opened Google, typed in *Bridgend suicide theories* and hit enter. After browsing down the results page he clicked to open a couple of links in new tabs. One of the first results to catch his eye was a forum thread from the

Fortean Times, a British magazine which focuses on strange phenomena.

The thread went into some discussion about one of the users' theory that the Bridgend suicides were the result of a 'Mosquito device', designed as a dispersal device, emitting ultra high frequencies and used to drive young people insane, thus taking their own lives. Even Ellis Flint, having plenty of form in being a sucker for the odd conspiracy theory, was not entirely taken in by this one. Like most conspiracy theories, this one didn't answer the most pertinent question: What would be the purpose?

Ellis's next Google result took him to David Icke's forum. As if the posters on the Fortean Times page hadn't seemed bonkers enough. The users on this forum were touting theories about ley lines and mobile phone masts, even going so far as to suggest that the masts were 'broadcasting kill-yourself frequencies' as one poster theorised. Ellis made a note on a piece of paper to do some further research on the possible effects of mobile phone masts.

Further down the thread, Ellis noted another reference to ley lines. This particular user had suggested that King Arthur's body is rumoured to have been buried in the Bridgend area, and that this might be a reason for some sort of curse or supernatural explanation. This appealed to Ellis's senses, and he made another note to research around this subject. He recalled the tale of the hauntings at the Manor Hotel and told himself he'd look further into that, too.

It was not often that Ellis Flint thought that other people had bizarre theories on life, but this morning he had already found the murkiest depths of the internet. Further posts from forum users threw up wild theories concerning wind farms, power stations and even government experiments or messages being sent by the Illuminati. Ellis liked the odd ghost story as much as the next man, and had always thought that there must be something to the world of the paranormal, but this lot were something else.

After all, Einstein said that every action must have an equal and opposite reaction, didn't he? He thought it was Einstein, anyway. Where did all of the energy and neural electricity go once someone had died? It couldn't just disappear. Ellis was feeling more and more certain that there could be a paranormal explanation to the suicides of Elliot Carr and Kimberly Gray. Had they heard about the hauntings at the Manor Hotel? Had they seen the ghost of the old woman? Had she told them to kill themselves? Was the place cursed?

There were too many questions for Ellis's alcohol- and caffeine-addled brain, and he was now suddenly feeling very tired. He closed his laptop lid, drank a pint of water and went back to bed for a couple of hours.

26

Later that morning, Kempston Hardwick once again found himself at South Heath station, waiting to get a train into London.

The journey by train, including the walks at either end, would take him over two hours each way, but Hardwick was not one for driving. He much preferred to sit on a train, staring out of the window as he processed his thoughts. Driving would require too much of his attention and distract him from thinking.

He had the journey planned out in his head already: he'd take the train down to St Pancras International, the Piccadilly line down to Holborn (he'd walk if the weather was good, but it wasn't) and then across to Greenford on the Central line. It was a long journey, but Hardwick felt it vital that he speak to Kimberly Gray's family and friends urgently. He was, by now, convinced that there was someone or something that needed stopping before any more lives were lost.

If someone had killed both Elliot Carr and Kimberly Gray, it would be finding a motive that would be most difficult. On the face of it, these two people seemed to be completely unconnected. Why would someone want to kill them both?

As the train pulled away from South Heath station, Hardwick's thoughts turned to Ellis Flint's theories. He'd mentioned something about a paranormal influence at the Manor Hotel. Hardwick was certainly not one for believing in ghost stories, but he couldn't help but wonder whether there might be some sort of psychosomatic influence at play. What if both Elliot Carr and Kimberly Gray had been aware of the stories about the Manor Hotel being haunted? What if they had thought they'd seen or heard something and this had led them to take their own lives?

Hardwick vaguely recalled reading something about this. Stressful situations, heightened awareness and even the presence of alcohol could all have contributed to both Elliot Carr's and Kimberly Gray's minds playing tricks on them. Elliot Carr had just had a row with his wife and had a few drinks. Kimberly Gray had just been at a concert to see her idol and had also had a few drinks. Could some form of hysteria be to blame here? It was possible, but Hardwick's nose for suspicion hadn't let him down yet and he was quite sure it wasn't doing so now.

He rolled an idea around in his head. What if Elliot and

Kimberly had somehow been drugged with something other than alcohol? He presumed the police will have ordered toxicology reports and addressed that already, but Hardwick knew he could never assume anything of Tollinghill Police. Some form of sedation would be a way of getting them up to room thirteen and onto the chair, though. However it was done, it would require a fair amount of strength — a well-built man, if not two, and in view of the hotel guests and staff. He made a mental note to mention this to Warner and perhaps have the toxicology reports looked at more closely.

As the rolling countryside gave way to the sprawling metropolis of London, Hardwick closed his eyes and ran through what he intended to ask Kimberly Gray's parents. He was sure the police would've already broached the obvious lines of questioning (Did she have a history of depression? Had she ever spoken about taking her own life? How did she seem when she left the house? What plans had she made for the future?) but he would need to ask them himself. DI Warner had been less than helpful so far, and he couldn't risk going back and confronting him again until he had some more concrete proof that something was amiss.

At just eighteen years of age, Kimberly was hardly likely to have confided too much in her parents, particularly on matters of a personal nature. At that age, she was far more likely to speak to her friends about any problems she might have had. As her friends were with her at the hotel on the night she died, they'd also have a far better idea as to her state of mind at the time, too, so Hardwick knew he'd have to find out the names and addresses of Kimberly's friends and speak to them.

This wasn't something he was looking forward to; he'd always found that people around their late teens made far better liars than adults. That was the age at which most lies were told, so it became second nature to them. An adult, with a wiser understanding of the world and knowing the full ramifications of even a little white lie, would be far more likely to give off small, barely noticeable signals when he or she was lying. Barely noticeable to most people, but not to Kempston Hardwick. After all, he had dedicated his life to searching for the truth and honing his skills in order to be able to catch those who had committed the ultimate sin.

The power of the subconscious was more evident than ever for Hardwick as he opened his eyes after what seemed like just a few seconds, but as the computerised female voice on the train announced that the train was just pulling in to St Pancras International. For one of the first times since hearing about the death of Elliot Carr, he'd fallen asleep.

27

Ellis woke up later that morning feeling bright and breezy. Incredible what an extra couple of hours' sleep could do to a hangover. He sat up, swung his legs out of bed, put on his clothes and headed downstairs to continue his online research. Having already looked into teenage suicide pacts earlier that day, he had opened up a number of other leads which he wanted to investigate.

First on his list was the subject of mobile phone masts and the effects they have on brainwaves. One theory being touted online was that this could be the reason why so many young people in Bridgend had taken their own lives over the past few years, with their brain waves being somehow affected by nearby mobile phone masts. Ellis didn't know where the nearest mobile phone mast was to the Manor Hotel, but he had made a note to look that up too.

He opened his web browser, went to Google and typed

in *mobile phone mast theories*. The number of results stunned him: almost half a million. One of the first websites was a news report on the theory that mobile phone masts were responsible for the decline in the British bee population, with the radiation from masts interfering with the bees' own in-built navigation senses.

Ellis added the word 'suicide' to the end of his search query and pressed enter. This time, there were even more results. One was a newspaper article written in 2008, which stated that a government advisor on mobile radiation had pointed out that all of the young people who killed themselves in Bridgend lived a lot closer to a mobile phone mast than the national average. The article stated that masts are, on average, eight hundred metres from residential homes in Britain. The Bridgend victims, however, lived just three hundred and fifty-six metres away on average.

He found a link from one article to a page on Ofcom's website which allowed users to enter their postcode and see which mobile phone masts were nearby. He entered the postcode for the Manor Hotel and navigated his way around the map.

He worked out that the nearest masts of any type were a Network Rail one on the train line, about 3,200 metres away and an O2 mobile phone mast a little closer but in the other direction. Surely too far away to have any major effect, he thought, seeing as both masts were about four times further away from the Manor Hotel than the national average. That theory would have to go on the back burner.

He crossed through the item on his list and looked at the next one. He'd written *King Arthur theory*, and had to take a few moments to try and recall what it was. Suddenly remembering, he typed *King Arthur theory Bridgend* into Google. He could only find a couple of passing references to the theory that King Arthur could have been buried in Bridgend, although most reputable sources he checked all stated that it couldn't be even said for definite that King Arthur ever existed.

This certainly wasn't Ellis's favourite theory. The complete lack of information meant that it could probably be discounted, plus even Ellis, who liked a ghost story better than most, could not quite see the logic in why people would start to commit suicide in an area in which a possibly mythical person might or might not have been buried 1,500 years ago.

That was not to say that Ellis didn't think there was some sort of paranormal explanation, though. The problems with hauntings at the Manor Hotel seemed to be well documented, particularly locally, and the supernatural events had taken place fairly recently — certainly in comparison with the King Arthur theory.

Ellis decided that the paranormal theory needed looking at more closely. This wasn't something he could broach with Kempston, though. He knew what his reaction would be. No, he needed something more concrete before he could bring the subject up again.

28

Hardwick was pleased to get off of the Underground and make the short walk from Greenford station to Kimberly Gray's parents' house. Hardwick was never keen on crowds, but he rather loved London. For him, the crowds were the only things that gave the city a sour air. He loved to people-watch and be around people, but had to balance that very carefully with his dislike of loud or crowded areas. This was not always an easy task.

After only a few minutes, he arrived at the address he'd found for the parents of Kimberly Gray and he used the brass knocker to rap loudly on the door, the handle squeaking and squealing as he did so.

Once again, as per usual, Hardwick was not asked to show any form of identification. He very rarely was, which he saw either as a sign that people really should take more care over who they speak to or that he perhaps carried with him an air of authority. There are those who say they can spot a police officer in a crowd. Hardwick thought that perhaps the amount of time he'd spent dealing with criminals and murderers might have given him that same beacon-like glow.

Once he'd introduced himself to Kimberly's parents, her mother offered him a cup of tea. Not just a cup of tea, but a choice of tea. Hardwick chose Earl Grey, naturally. He sipped at the steaming cup as they all shuffled into the living room and sat down on the three sofas.

He noted that Kimberly's mother, who'd introduced herself as Katherine (with a K), seemed to be a Type B mourner: the type that copes with grief by trying to carry on as normal, even coming across as uncaring or aloof. Hardwick, despite all signs to the contrary, did not like being around grieving people and much preferred this Type B mourner.

Kimberly's dad, Tony (with a T), on the other hand, seemed really rather subdued. Then again, it was entirely possible that he was always like this. Behaviours and quirks of character were the sorts of things that Hardwick tended to notice quite quickly, and it was often these traits which had been the downfall of suspects in the past.

'We're not really quite sure what we can say,' Katherine said, her voice clipped and refined. The product of her private education at Wycombe Abbey School for Girls, Hardwick thought, having already done his research — mostly through Facebook, of course. Gone were the days of having to delve through records and follow a paper trail. These days, everyone seemed quite happy to put their entire life story on Facebook, making Hardwick's job much easier as a result. He had resisted using it for a long time, and technically still didn't use it. Not under his own name, anyway; he now had a range of aliases and means for finding out information using the social networking site.

'I just need to take down as much detail as you know,' Hardwick said, not wanting to give away the content of any of his questions until he'd asked them. That way, he could observe Katherine and Tony's body language as they first heard the question and then responded to it.

'We've already told the other officers everything we know,' Tony replied. Ah, yes, Hardwick thought, noticing that her husband's voice gave away his schooling background, too: Slough Comprehensive. 'Don't you lot ever talk to each other?' Ah. The angry griever, Hardwick thought.

'We just need to clarify a few details to make sure everything we've noted is accurate,' Hardwick said, noticing Tony Gray's eyebrows rising by a good few millimetres. 'Firstly, if it's not too upsetting, I'd just like to find out a little more about Kimberly's general manner and state of mind in the days and weeks leading up to her death, if I may.'

'She seemed absolutely fine,' her mother replied. 'She was very excited about going to the concert, of course. She'd been wanting to see Alex Alvarez for ages, but this was his first UK tour so was the first chance she'd had. It was her birthday recently, her eighteenth, so she'd had a great time then. She'd just passed her driving test, too. She had absolutely nothing to be upset about. We bought her the concert tickets and the hotel room as a birthday treat.'

'And she drove there with her friends, didn't she?' Hardwick asked, Katherine Gray nodding. 'Was it her own car?'

'Yes,' she replied.

'She bought it with her own money,' Tony added. 'Went out, got a job and saved up.' Hardwick noted the glance that Tony and Katherine gave each other. It was a glance that said *And that's the way things are done in the real world, love.*

'So there was absolutely no sign that anything was bothering her at all?' Hardwick asked, trying to lighten the atmosphere but failing miserably.

'No, not at all,' Katherine replied.

'Would she have confided in you had she had something on her mind, do you think?' Hardwick said.

'Oh, I don't know. Quite possibly not. You know what teenagers are like,' she replied. 'I should imagine they've got all sorts of secrets. I know I did at that age.'

'Do you think she might have confided in a friend?' Hardwick asked. 'Is there one friend she felt particularly close to?'

'Possibly. Her two closest friends, Rhiannon and Charlotte both went to the concert with her. I suppose if there was anything she had been worried or upset about, she'd've told them.'

Hardwick enquired as to Rhiannon and Charlotte's surnames and addresses and noted them down.

'And, of course, they would've seen her most recently, just before she... you know... so they might have a bit more of an idea,' Katherine said.

Hardwick nodded. He always thought it odd how people were sometimes unwilling or unable to say 'died'. It was particularly noticeable with suicides, with many people not liking the S-word. True enough, it had the connotations of crime, which was quite an undesirable and unfortunate thing. *Committing suicide* sounds more like a criminal act than the last resort of someone tortured and troubled to the depths of despair, to the point where they feel their only way out is to end their life. However, Hardwick was quite sure that in the cases of Elliot Carr and Kimberly Gray, a crime had indeed been committed. Not suicide, but murder.

'And she'd been getting on well at work, had she?' Hardwick asked.

'Oh yes,' Katherine said. 'Just a part-time job, you know, but she'd been enjoying it. They were starting to increase her hours, as well, which was good. They said once she'd finished her exams they'd be willing to offer her a full-time place. I don't know if she would have taken it or not. She'd spoken about perhaps taking a year or so to build up some money before going to university.'

'Oh? What was she going to study?' Kempston asked.

'She wasn't sure', Katherine replied. 'She'd thought about maybe doing psychology or even English Lit.'

Hardwick nodded. It had always riled him that tens of thousands of young people every year were shepherded out of school and into university for no good reason. Young people with no plans, landed with thirty-thousand pounds worth of debt and a degree they don't know if they'll ever use. And all so that the schools could say *X% of our students go on to university*.

'And you mentioned that she had been working. What was she doing?'

'She was working for an advertising company in town,' Tony said. 'Starting to build up a name for herself in the company, too.'

Hardwick left a couple of moments' silence before changing the subject again. 'This might sound a little odd, but did Kimberly ever mention seeing any news items about the death of a man called Elliot Carr?'

Kimberly's parents looked at each other. 'I don't think so,' her mother said. 'The name doesn't ring a bell anyway. Why?'

'Because Elliot Carr also died at the Manor Hotel, just over a week ago. And the verdict was suicide then, too.'

'But surely lots of people die in hotels,' Tony interrupted. 'Doesn't mean anything, surely?'

'Usually I'd agree with you. But there are a number of similarities between the deaths of your daughter and Elliot Carr.'

'Such as?'

'Such as the fact that they both died from hanging. In the same room. And both using dressing gown cords.'

Neither of Kimberly's parents spoke a word for a good twenty seconds. Hardwick opted not to speak either, giving them time to process this new information as he watched their faces carefully.

It was Katherine who finally broke the silence. 'Do you... Do you think Kimberly might have been... killed?'

'If I'm completely honest,' Hardwick said, 'I don't know. As I said, there are some remarkable similarities between the two deaths. There could be any number of reasons for that, though.'

'Such as?'

'Well, you have to bear in mind that I'm not necessarily saying that this is what happened, but there have been instances in the past of young people taking their own lives in the same way as others have before, in so-called copycat suicides.' Kimberly's parents looked shocked and upset. 'Of course, as I said I'm not saying that's what happened in this case. It's just one theory which could explain it. It could be a complete coincidence, too, although I personally think that's unlikely. So I'm afraid I have to ask. Do you know of anyone who had fallen out with Kimberly? Perhaps someone who had a grudge of some sort?'

'No, definitely not,' Katherine said. 'She had so many friends and was very popular. I can't remember her ever even telling me about having an argument with anyone, let alone something like this.'

'If... If she has been... murdered,' Tony said, stuttering slightly, 'do you think it might be one of these random killers? Maybe it's just someone who kills people randomly because they enjoy it. You see it on the TV all the time.'

'And I'm afraid that's largely where it stays,' Hardwick

says. 'That's extraordinarily rare. On the whole, all killers have a reason for choosing the victims they choose. They need some sort of validation or justification in their mind for killing. It's very rare for people to just kill indiscriminately. To be honest, the pure coincidence theory is probably more likely.'

'But how can you just dismiss it like that?' Tony asked. 'If there's even the slightest possibility that there's a madman out there killing innocent people at random, shouldn't you do something about it?'

'That's just the problem,' Hardwick said. 'Not only is it extremely unlikely, but it'd also be very difficult to find them unless they were already known to the police, as there would be very little, if anything, to connect them to the killings.'

Both Katherine and Tony were silent for a few moments before Katherine finally spoke, softly. 'So what you're saying is that there's no hope?'

'No,' Hardwick replied. 'What I'm saying is that I'll do everything I can to help you find out what happened to Kimberly. But it won't be easy.'

29

Unable to concentrate on doing much else, Ellis had been back to the Manor Hotel to "get into the zone" as he called it. If he was being truthful to himself, he was still hugely intrigued by the paranormal theories surrounding the place.

He'd spoken to the hotel's manager who'd told him that bookings had dropped off since the news had got out about the second suicide and the local newspaper, the Tollinghill Echo, had gone to press with a story theorising that the deaths were somehow linked and that there was some strange cultish effect going on locally. Unsurprisingly, the hotel's manager wasn't best pleased about this.

Fortunately for Ellis, though, he did understand the potential marketing angle for a supernatural theory. He knew from his predecessors just how valuable the story of the ghost at the Manor Hotel had been in people coming to stay at the hotel, and shortly after it was featured on the television in the mid-1990s, the hotel had been booked out solidly for the next six months. Unsurprisingly, then, he was particularly keen on Ellis's idea that they should hold a paranormal investigation at the hotel.

Whereas across the pond in America a haunted house or hotel would be a huge downfall, with houses losing tens of thousands of dollars off their value if it's suspected there's a ghost, in the UK a good haunting could be a gold-mine. It would certainly be a far better marketing angle than being the home of the country's latest suicide cult, anyway. As such, the manager was keen that a paranormal investigation be carried out as soon as possible.

Ellis, too, was keen that things should get underway quickly, so he'd called the Shafford & District Paranormal Society from the hotel to see if they'd be interested. They'd said that they did an investigation at the hotel almost fifteen years ago and had been due to visit again soon, but with the story being in the news now would be the perfect time to set up an investigation.

'We've got to strike while the iron's hot,' the society's president, Robin Joyce, had said. 'The fact of the matter is, if the last death was only a couple of days ago, the activity in the area will probably still be pretty high. Unsurprisingly, there's a lot of residual energy left when someone dies, particularly if it was a violent death. If we're going to see any activity, it'll be now.'

Even Ellis was surprised at just how quickly they'd sprung into action, with an investigation planned for that same evening. Robin had told him that paranormal activity often comes in waves, and if the deaths at the hotel had been paranormal in their origins then that would indicate that they were currently riding the crest of a wave and needed to get in fast.

30

After leaving Kimberly's parents' house, Hardwick had called Kimberly's friends, Rhiannon and Charlotte, and asked them to meet him at a local coffee shop.

Hardwick arrived before them, and was already sipping on his strong black coffee when he saw the two girls walking arm-in-arm through the automatic sliding doors. He stood and extended his hand to greet them.

'Kempston Hardwick. You must be Rhiannon and Charlotte,' he said, knowing damn well that they were as he'd looked them up on Facebook so he'd recognise them when they arrived.

'Yes, hi,' said Rhiannon. 'I was going to ask if you wanted us to get you a coffee, but I see you've already got one.'

'Yes, I have, thank you,' Hardwick replied, turning back to his notepad.

'We'll... go and get our own, then, shall we?' Charlotte said, probing.

'Okay, yes,' Hardwick replied.

Rhiannon muttered something under her breath as the pair went to order their drinks before joining Hardwick back at his table. He was scribbling furiously in his notebook, which he snapped shut once he'd realised Rhiannon and Charlotte were back at the table.

'Do we have to give another formal statement or something?' Charlotte asked. 'Only we've already done two. One up in South Heath and another one here.'

'Oh no, nothing like that,' Hardwick replied, trying to force a smile. 'Just a couple of questions to tie up loose ends, you know. To try and find some closure for the family.'

'I understand. Her parents seem really cut up about it,' Rhiannon said, noticing Hardwick's raised eyebrow. 'Well, obviously her mum is her mum. She's always been like that, but believe me she's gutted. She just puts on a brave face and tries to get on with things. Not always the best way, though, is it? I mean, you've got to grieve at some point, haven't you?'

'Indeed,' Hardwick replied. 'How long had you both known Kimberly? Long enough to get to know her parents, I see.'

'Oh yes. Yeah, we've been at school together for years. Since juniors for me, and Charlotte joined us at secondary.'

'Have you always been close?' Hardwick asked.

'Yeah, really close,' Rhiannon said, tears starting to form in her eyes. 'We used to tell each other everything.'

'So you would've known if something had been on her mind in the days and weeks leading up to her death?' Hardwick asked. 'Something which would've made her want to take her own life.'

'Definitely. She would've told me. But there was nothing. She'd just turned eighteen, passed her driving test and we'd just seen Alex Alvarez. I'd never seen her so happy. But you never know, do you?'

'Very true,' Hardwick said, quickly running out of angles of attack. 'Now, this might sound a little bit odd to you, but please humour me. Were either of you, or Kimberly, aware of rumours or stories that the Manor Hotel was haunted?'

Rhiannon let out an involuntary laugh. 'Are you serious? To answer your question, no, we weren't, but what has that got to do with anything?'

'Are you seriously suggesting that a ghost killed Kimberly or something? Because if you are, I want to have a word with your superior. You must be mad.'

'No no,' Hardwick said. 'I think you've got it all wrong, I—'

'Your lot just don't want to know,' Charlotte said. 'You'll come up with any excuse just to get the paperwork shoved through more quickly. Whatever the easiest option is. Suicide, accident and now killer ghosts, for Christ's sake. They keep saying that there was probably something she just didn't want to tell us. But we know that's not true. Kimberly never hid anything from us.'

Hardwick sighed before he spoke. It wasn't often he did this unless he had to, but he felt it would be beneficial in this instance. 'I'm not actually a police officer. And no, I'm not a journalist or anything like that. I am investigating Kimberly's death, just like I said. I'm a private investigator. And before you close ranks, I just want you to know that I'm on your side here. Like you said, the police just aren't interested. They're convinced that Kimberly's death was a suicide, but I know — just as you do — that it wasn't. Now, I promise I'll get to the bottom of what happened that night at the Manor Hotel. But I can only do that if you'll help me.'

There was a few moments' silence before Rhiannon and Charlotte both looked at each other without saying any words, in the way only old and close friends could.

'Yes,' Rhiannon said, nodding. 'We'll help you.'

31

Having looked up a contact for the South Heath Local History Society, Ellis had called and arranged to meet a man called Graham Simpson, who told him he knew quite a lot about the hauntings at the Manor Hotel and could meet him late that afternoon at the Freemason's Arms in Tollinghill. That would give him plenty of time to get back down to South Heath in time for the paranormal investigation.

Ellis ordered a pint of his favourite beer, Pheasant Plucker, and sat down at a small table near the front window. Fortunately for him, Graham Simpson's photo was on the South Heath Local History Society website, so he hoped he would recognise him when he arrived.

Just a few minutes later, Graham Simpson did arrive and Ellis did recognise him. The man's bushy white moustache curled upwards as he smiled and shook Ellis's hand. Once Ellis had bought him a drink, he sat down and launched straight into what he knew about the odd goings-on at the Manor Hotel.

'It really is quite a spooky story,' Graham said. 'In fact, ITV featured it on one of their paranormal programmes nearly twenty years ago. They even had interviews with the people who'd seen and heard things, which always lends a little more credibility to the reports. Usually it's just a case of a bloke in a pub telling someone that they heard something from someone else. That's how these things get blown out of proportion. But with the Manor Hotel, we have the benefit of knowing exactly who saw what and when.'

Ellis leaned in a little closer, sensing that Graham Simpson's intellect and local knowledge could be very handy indeed.

'Now, the Manor Hotel — or South Heath Manor as it was called before it was a hotel — was built in the early 1800s as a private house for a chap called John Moreton. After he died, it passed down through the family until it was sold in the 1990s, when it became a hotel.'

'It'd stayed in the family all that time?' Ellis asked.

'Absolutely. Big houses like that nowadays are far too expensive to keep running. That's why so many become hotels or end up going to English Heritage. Now, the story behind the hauntings is linked to the early 1900s. What do you know so far?'

'Something about an elderly housekeeper who was accused of poisoning a child. Is that right?' Ellis asked, feeling proud of himself as Graham nodded.

'Yep, that's about it. The woman was called Mrs Fletcher. There's a record of her on one of the censuses, and then on the next one she's just not there. Her death certificate shows that she didn't die for a little while, so the presumption is that she was sacked. Now, this is where the story ties in. As you say, the rumour was that she had been trying to poison one of the children in the household and was sacked for it. In between the census that shows Mrs Fletcher living at South Heath Manor and the one that doesn't, there is indeed a record of a child dying at the manor. Their infant son, George. So although there's not a complete paper trail, it does seem that the rumours fit around what we do know as facts.'

'So you're comfortable enough from your own research to say that it actually happened?' Ellis asked, before taking a sip of his beer.

'Well, don't quote me on that. But it's one of the stronger cases of local legend, let's put it that way. Now, when the manor was converted into a hotel, that's when things started to go a bit odd. As you might know, in manor houses the housekeepers tended to live on the very top floor. That's the area where the storage room now is at the hotel and where the two people died recently. That room was only revealed to exist when the builders came in to renovate for the hotel firm. The timelines indicate that the room was bricked up after Mrs Fletcher left but before the manor became a hotel. I wouldn't be surprised if, after Mrs Fletcher died, phenomena at the manor meant that someone bricked up the room in order to stop her spirit from wandering. If you believe in that sort of thing, that is.'

Ellis nodded. He certainly did believe in that sort of thing. 'And it wasn't opened again until the builders came in twenty years ago?' he asked.

'So the story goes. After the room was discovered, the hotel owners opened it up and turned it into the thirteenth room. Now, what have you heard or read about what happened afterwards?' Graham sat back and took a long drink of his beer.

'Well,' Ellis said, 'I heard that the receptionist was staying at the hotel one night and she woke up and saw an old woman in her room. And a businessman had a similar thing happen to him too.'

'Yep. The sighting of an old woman is actually pretty common. Guests and staff have all said the same thing. Some have even seen her face and described her as upset or distraught. Now, I'm not necessarily one for believing in the paranormal, but all of these people have said pretty much the same thing. It makes sense in that case that the woman they're seeing is Mrs Fletcher, who's distraught at having been sacked from her job. Of course, she had been confined to her room until the wall was taken down and she was allowed to roam.'

'Do we know if there were any other stories from before it became a hotel?' Ellis asked. 'Did nothing happen at all while it was in private hands?'

'Not quite as much, no. Although some of the family who owned it last are still around and they've mentioned having heard footsteps coming from above them at night, and odd noises. Not what you'd expect, seeing as there are no other houses around them. Just the church. Most of the stories are from since it was opened as a hotel, though. A lot of people won't set foot in the place again. Many won't even talk about what they've seen.'

'One bloke who worked there, an Owen Bartlett, actually handed in his resignation and walked straight out on the night Elliot Carr committed suicide,' Ellis said, starting to form a theory in his head. 'Do you reckon he might have seen the old lady and had to leave, there and then?'

'That's something you'll have to ask him,' Graham said.

32

That evening, Ellis arrived at the Manor Hotel to see three cars parked next to each other outside the front of the hotel, with a group of people ferrying equipment from the boots and back seats of the cars and into the reception room of the hotel.

Ellis wasn't sure which one was Robin Joyce, so he headed into reception to find the hotel's manager, whose name he either hadn't remembered or still hadn't asked. Well, you couldn't really ask him *now*, after having spent half the morning chatting to him, could you?

'Ah, Ellis!' the manager said, clearly having remembered his name. 'Good to see you. To be honest, it's the perfect night for it. Our last two bookings for this evening both cancelled at lunchtime. For the first time since I've been here, we're completely empty tonight.'

'Looks like we've got free reign, then,' a man carrying a

camera stand said, extending his free hand towards Ellis. 'Robin Joyce. We spoke on the phone.'

'Ah, yes. Good to meet you,' Ellis said. 'Do you need a hand with anything?' he said, gesturing with his thumb over his shoulder towards the cars outside.

'No, but thanks for asking. The guys know where everything needs to go and they get a bit tetchy if people start touching their gear. Thousands of pounds worth and it's not worth the hassle, to be honest. Quicker just to let them get on with it.'

'Sure, no problem,' Ellis said, not really fancying any heavy lifting anyway. 'I'll wait for you in the bar, then. First drink's on me when you're done setting up.'

Ellis sat in the bar with his pint of beer as he watched the sun setting over the manor grounds through the impressive french windows. It had always baffled him how some of the residents of Tollinghill sneered at South Heath, but the countryside surrounding Tollinghill was nothing compared to this.

Around half an hour later, Robin Joyce joined Ellis in the bar and introduced him to the rest of the team.

'This is Dave Sansom,' he said, gesturing to a large man with long, straggly dark hair and an unkempt beard. 'He's our EMF man. He keeps an eye on the electro-magnetic fields, which can fluctuate when there's a paranormal presence. Lucie Greene, she's our EVP expert. That's the sound angle, if you like. We've found that ghosts try to communicate with us audibly, but that the frequencies often aren't picked up by the ears of the living. Her EVP recorders pick that up. And Ajit Patel is our man with the thermal cam, if you'd pardon my little rhyme,' Robin said, chuckling at his own joke. 'He'll be looking out for cold spots and areas of thermal fluctuation. He's put cameras up all over the hotel, and they'll be focused on areas where there've been lots of reports of paranormal activity.'

'And yourself?' Ellis asked.

'I oversee everything and tend to be pretty perceptive when it comes to sensing paranormal presences. I tend to be more able to see physical forms of ghosts and even hear them sometimes. Not everyone has that gift, but those who do are usually the poor unsuspecting souls who have the paranormal experiences in their own homes or while staying in places like this. That's why some people will go their whole lives believing in ghosts but never seeing or experiencing anything and others will be the world's biggest skeptics but still experience strange phenomena and have experiences which they just can't explain any other way. Quite a lot of them are converted to being believers, funnily enough.'

'So you've seen things yourself?' Ellis asked, feeling a tingling sensation running down his spine as the hairs on the back of his neck stood up. This was just his sort of evening.

'Oh yes. Many times. That's not to say that I experience something in every location, of course. As I said to you earlier, these things tend to fluctuate and come in waves, so it might be that there's no activity at all tonight. When our group came fifteen years ago, which was before my time, the reports say there was quite a bit of activity early on in the evening when the crew were setting up their equipment, but that it was pretty uneventful after that. Sometimes the ghosts just don't want to play.'

'And if they do?' Ellis asked, leaning in towards Robin. 'What could happen? I mean, could it be dangerous?'

'There's always a danger, of course,' Robin said, sensing Ellis's worry. 'Largely, ghosts are harmless and are just trying to communicate and not to hurt anyone. Of course, there are also poltergeists and forms of spirit which do try to actively cause harm. If the recent events at the hotel are anything to go by, and if they were caused by the ghosts, then it could well be that there's an element of danger, yes. That's why we're going to move around as a group as opposed to splitting off as we might do otherwise.'

Ellis nodded vigorously, trying not to seem to excited, but at the same time anxious and eager to get the evening's ghost hunting underway.

The staff at the hotel had been instructed to carry on as they usually would, despite the lack of guests that night. Hotel business needed to carry on as normally as possible in order for the investigation to be carried out effectively.

The bar and lounge was designated as the meeting point and headquarters for the investigation, with two large computer monitors set up on a central table, where live footage from Ajit's cameras could be viewed. Cameras had been set up in the main entrance, rooms seven and eight, both of which were directly under room thirteen and had been involved in reports of paranormal activity, room thirteen itself and the upper staircase leading up to it. The team would also concentrate on these areas throughout the investigation, using their EMF and EVP meters as well as a range of other types of equipment.

The bar area itself would be left largely alone, with the thermal video footage from each of the areas left to record should anything need to be watched back. Ajit would be with the rest of the crew with a small handheld thermal imaging camera which he would carry from room to room, looking for warm or cold areas or sudden temperature fluctuations.

Ellis was in his element and he wished that Hardwick could be here to see how much effort and science went into the art of ghost hunting, but he could almost predict Hardwick's words were he to even suggest it. It wasn't the sort of idea he'd entertain and he'd doubtless have something to criticise on the scientific side of things, too. Cold, hard proof is what he needed. Ellis, though, just wanted some sort of lead or spark of inspiration which could help lead him towards a credible theory behind the deaths of Elliot Carr and Kimberly Gray. A theory which would stand up to the Hardwick test.

The crew headed towards room seven, which was where the investigation would begin. Room seven was where Elliot Carr had been staying, and was situated directly beneath room thirteen, which was the room in which he died. A lot of activity had been reported in and around this room over the years, including the incidents involving one of the hotel's first receptionists and the travelling businessman, both of whom had independently seen the ghost of an old woman crying at the end of their bed.

Ellis was excited yet apprehensive about heading up to room seven. Going in during the daytime with the lights on wasn't a problem, but heading up there in the dead of night with a bunch of people who were actively trying to find ghosts gave the whole situation a completely different feel. Ellis's senses were heightened and he knew that if he was ever going to see or experience something, tonight would be the night.

Shortly after midnight, Ellis, Ajit, Dave and Robin were walking through the reception area, having come down from upstairs, when a loud crashing sound was heard coming from the kitchen area.

When they arrived in the kitchen, the scene that greeted them was an entire cutlery tray upturned on the floor, a sea of knives, forks and spoons spread across the tiles.

'Hello?' Robin called out. 'Is anyone around?'

Silence greeted them.

Dave waved his EMF meter in the air, slowly shaking his head and pushing his bottom lip out. 'Nothing on the EMF. Must've been a pretty big disturbance.'

'That cutlery tray was on the counter there, held in that recess,' Ellis said, pointing to the two-inch deep rectangular dip in the counter. 'It was there when we started earlier and I don't think anyone else has been down here. There's no way it could just lift itself out of the recess and tip over.'

'Have we got cameras on the kitchen?' Robin asked Ajit.

'Afraid not,' Ajit replied. 'Only on the bedrooms where stuff's been reported before and the upper staircase. Nothing down here.'

'Damn.'

'Would Lucy have picked something up on her sound gear?' Ellis asked.

'Well yeah, a bloody great cutlery tray smashing to the ground,' Ajit replied, the resultant laughter breaking the tense atmosphere somewhat. 'Seriously, though, there's no record of any activity on the downstairs level here at all in the past. Everything has been in the guest rooms upstairs, which is why we concentrated there. If we're getting activity downstairs then that's pretty worrying.'

'Is it?' Ellis asked. 'Why's that?'

Ajit blinked and looked at Ellis, his face the very definition of seriousness. 'Because it means that whatever's here is getting angrier.'

TUESDAY 24TH MARCH

33

Kit Daniels sat at his desk in the office of the Tollinghill Echo, glancing a final eye over his masterpiece. The story of the Bridgend suicides a few years ago had become national, even international, news and he knew the potential of the story he had here with the incidents happening at the Manor Hotel in South Heath.

He'd been fortunate enough to have a few stories sold up to the nationals over his time at the Echo, including a sex scandal involving the local Member of Parliament and a leaked memo regarding the installation of a huge wind farm on the edge of Shafford. Each time a national paper had picked up a story of his, he received a nice little bonus from the editor, who in turn had received a juicy payout from the national.

It was the quickest and easiest way of making money on the local paper and the stories didn't even have to be necessarily accurate. If the story was deemed to be in the public interest or had sufficient witness testimony, no matter how unreliable the witnesses, it was often the case that the subjects of stories would almost never bring about legal action against the Echo. If they did, it was unlikely they'd win the case and if they did the compensation would be a drop in the ocean compared to the money each story made them in the first place. And a potential suicide scandal would make a *lot* of money.

Kit knew only too well that the lower rungs of the journalism ladder didn't tend to deliver much in the way of a salary. Even with three years on the paper and the enormous number of hours he put in, he was still taking home little more than a postman. He'd often wondered whether that would have been a better career choice. Finish at lunchtime, get a bit of exercise in the morning while doing the round. Would help shift the slight paunch which was developing around his waist, too. That was another drawback to working in an office: there was always someone who'd bring in cakes or chocolates, and it'd be rude to say no.

If this story really hit the big time, Kit knew it could be the making of him. He'd almost certainly have enough money to finally tip his savings account over the line at which point mortgage advisors would actually bother to give him the time of day, which would help keep his girlfriend, Becky, happy. She'd been on at him for months about finally getting a place together but she just didn't understand how these things worked.

He'd told her they'd need to save up for a deposit and

not keep spending money on stupid things like clothes and nights out, but she wouldn't have it. She said she'd looked into it and they could rent a place and only need a month's rent money as a deposit. It was dead money, he'd told her, and they'd be far better off waiting and getting a place of their own. So far, he'd managed to hold her off but he knew that would only last so long. At some point, a decision had to be made. With the story on the screen in front of him, though, he could have his answer.

Kit knew exactly what the reaction would be. From the public, it would be sheer hysteria. The usual bored old housewives and retired men would be calling and writing in to demand that the hotel be closed, the mobile phone masts ripped down and everyone given a nine o'clock curfew. The hotel owners would be up in arms saying it was giving them bad publicity, and statistics showed that people died in hotels all the time and it was perfectly normal, thank you very much. *Try telling that to their families*, he'd reply. And Detective Inspector Rob Warner would be straight on the phone to accuse him of interfering in police work.

He knew the pattern. It was always the same when Kit reported on local crime stories, which he often did. Three years service was quite a long time for a local newspaper, and he was now in a position to claim *de facto* any crime stories which passed through the news desk. Whether it be a murder or just a burglary or even the holy grail: an elderly person being beaten up by a youth, he would be all over it like a rash. Crime stories shifted papers and were much easier to sell up to the nationals. As with everything, it all came back to money.

Kit knew that two deaths at one hotel was hardly a 'suicide scandal', but his sources had tipped him off as to an extra few details. Both Elliot Carr and Kimberly Gray had died in the same room, were unknown to each other and both hanged themselves with a dressing gown cord. This was the sort of story which could carry on momentum for a long time, so he would continue to keep an eye on the place and big-up any odd occurrences at the hotel, no matter how seemingly insignificant.

For now, though, this story would get the ball rolling perfectly.

34

'Ellis? It's me,' Hardwick said as he barked into the payphone near the train station in South Heath. 'Listen, I'm going to pop down to Brighton and chat to Owen Bartlett myself. I need to know why he left so suddenly that night. Something isn't quite right.'

'You're a mind reader, Kempston. Last night I was speaking to a local historian and something popped into my mind about Owen. Can you ask him something for me?' Ellis was sure he could hear Hardwick sighing on the other end of the phone.

'What is it, Ellis?'

'Can you ask him if he ran off because he saw the ghost of Mrs Fletcher?'

Hardwick was silent for a few moments. 'Ellis, this is no time for messing around. Can you just give me Owen's address? I wrote it down but left the piece of paper in my kitchen. Can you remember where he lives?'

'Oh yes, I remember,' Ellis said.

'Good. Where is it?'

'That all depends,' Ellis said, smirking. 'Will you ask him about the ghost of Mrs Fletcher?'

'Ellis, this isn't something we can be foolish with. People have died and you're still mucking about with your silly paranormal theories. Will you just leave it be and give me Owen Bartlett's address so I can speak to him?'

'I will if you'll ask him the question,' Ellis replied.

'Ellis, there's no need to blackmail me. I'm quite happy to find an internet café and look up his address myself if you're going to play the fool.' Hardwick sounded incredibly exasperated now.

'Do it for me as a friend, then,' Ellis said. The line went silent, but he knew Hardwick hadn't hung up because he could still hear the traffic from Greenford high street. 'I am your friend, aren't I?' he said, knowing that Hardwick never admitted to anyone being a friend. *Colleague* or *acquaintance* was the closest he ever came when being introduced to people.

'Ellis, can I have the address please.'

'Will you ask him?'

Hardwick sighed audibly again. 'Yes, Ellis. I'll ask him.'

With the address written down, Hardwick left the phone box and headed down the steps to the station platform. This amount of travelling on trains was starting to get to him. The operator on the line that ran through South Heath was less than reliable, to say the least, but up until now his journeys had been fairly smooth and delay-free.

He crossed his fingers that it'd continue in that vein today as he had a four-hour round trip to Brighton to deal with.

Sat in his seat on the train, he leant his head back and allowed himself to drift into a light sleep as the train pulled away from the station and headed south towards London and the coastal town of Brighton.

A thousand and one thoughts swirled through his head. He was not one to give up easily, but even he was now starting to doubt himself. Was he chasing a lost cause? Was there really anything suspicious behind the deaths of Elliot Carr and Kimberly Gray? Or was he potentially causing more harm than good? He knew that theoretically there was no reason for either of them to have been killed but also that neither of them were the type of people to want to kill themselves. Yet both were dead.

Above all, he knew something wasn't right. There was an injustice somewhere along the line and injustices were things Hardwick could not abide. He had experienced enough injustices in his life to convince him that he would make sure he did everything he could to prevent more. Every time there was someone thinking they could get away with taking away people's lives and ruining the lives of others for their own personal gain, so too would he be there to stop them.

35

Hardwick knocked on the door at St George's Terrace in Brighton and waited for an answer. He could hear the seagulls cawing in the distance and the chatter of excited children crowding towards the seafront, even a couple of blocks away from the front as he was now.

That was just one of the many things Hardwick had always liked about Brighton: it was constantly moving. They say that New York is the city that never sleeps, but Brighton is quite possibly England's closest equivalent. Even the centre of London goes eerily quiet in the early hours, but there's always life somewhere in Brighton.

After a few seconds, the door opened and Hardwick was greeted by a young, meek looking man. He looked unassuming and lamblike as he stood here before Hardwick, almost a good foot shorter than the detective and with eyes which showed absolutely no confidence whatsoever.

'Yes?' he said, having not expected Hardwick's visit.

'Hello. My name's Kempston Hardwick. Are you Owen Bartlett?'

'Yes, why?' Owen answered, seeming highly suspicious.

'There's nothing to worry about,' Hardwick said, trying to put the lad at ease. 'I just need to speak to you to find out some information about an incident at the Manor Hotel in South Heath. You're not in any trouble; I just need some information. May I come in?'

Owen said nothing, but nodded and stepped aside to let Hardwick into the hallway before gesturing towards the living room. Hardwick walked through and noticed the decor was a little less than conventional, which Owen clearly noticed.

'It's my mum. She's into all the new-age hippy stuff. It's all harmless, but I guess some people find it a bit weird,' Owen said. He didn't exactly have an air of convention about himself either, Hardwick thought. 'Would you like a cup of tea?'

'That would be lovely, thanks,' Hardwick said. 'I shan't keep you long.'

As Owen scurried off to the kitchen to make tea, Hardwick took a slow saunter around the living room, inspecting the photographs on display. There were a couple of Owen, some of another young man and some of them both together with a lady who Hardwick assumed to be their mother.

On the walls hung hessian designs and a variety of

dreamcatchers. The room smelt heavily of joss sticks and something which Hardwick faintly recognised as cannabis. He smiled as he realised just how strangely comfortable he felt here.

His own parents had been unconventional creatures, two of the earliest mainstream climate change scientists who had tried to change public opinion towards accepting the facts surrounding climate change. His father had, for a while, been involved in revolutionary politics in South America whilst working in Chile. The smell of joss sticks in Owen Bartlett's living room brought back many memories, some happy and some far less so.

The tea made, Owen appeared back in the living room.

'We don't have any sugar, I'm afraid. And the milk's almond. Hope that's okay.'

'Not a problem at all,' Hardwick said. 'In fact, I prefer it. Mammals aren't designed to ingest milk after they've been weaned. Everyone who puts milk in their tea is abusing their digestive system, as far as I'm concerned.'

'Well, I think she just prefers the taste,' Owen said, handing Hardwick his cup.

They sat down in silence for a few moments before Hardwick started speaking.

'How long were you working at the Manor Hotel?'

'Probably just getting on for a year,' Owen replied.

'It's a long way to go, though, isn't it?' Hardwick asked, having long wondered why a young man from Brighton would choose to work in South Heath.

'Well yeah, it is. I was working at Markham Grange,

just up the road, which is owned by the Belvedere group, same as who own the Manor in South Heath. I'd kinda had enough of Brighton and wanted to see a bit more of Britain so I asked if they could transfer me to another hotel. A friend of mine did something similar a few months before so I knew that they'd usually put you up in one of the rooms, too, so you get your accommodation thrown in. If they give you the transfer, that is. Luckily they said they could move me to South Heath, but couldn't guarantee a room would be available all the time. I went anyway, and ended up lodging nearby.'

'And after you left the Manor Hotel you came back here to stay with your mother?' Hardwick asked.

'Yeah, that's right.'

'Is she in at the moment?' Hardwick asked.

'No, she's out shopping,' Owen replied.

'Oh, feeling better is she?' Hardwick noticed that Owen's face had a look of confusion. 'Only I was told that you left South Heath because you had to come back and look after your mother because she was ill.'

'Ah. Well, yes, she—'

'It's fine. Trust me, it's much easier if you just tell the truth. Most things are entirely innocent if you let them be,' Hardwick said, interrupting him.

'What's innocent about running off just after someone dies?' Owen said, almost laughing.

'You tell me. Why did you leave? Honestly.'

'Because I couldn't bear to be there any more. I just had to go. I'd not enjoyed working there for a while and that was just the final straw for me. Do you know what it's like when something like that happens? It's horrible. I just didn't want to be there any more. I wanted to be here, back home, and start again.'

'You must be able to see how that looks to other people, though?' Hardwick asked.

'Well yeah, obviously.'

'You're quite lucky the coroner agreed it was suicide. Otherwise you'd have absconded from the scene of a crime and would be arrested.'

'Yeah... I know,' Owen said. 'Sorry.'

'No need to apologise,' Hardwick said. 'I just need to get the facts in order. Do you remember which train you got back to Brighton?'

'Uh... I can't remember what time it left South Heath. Is it important?'

'Possibly not,' Hardwick said. 'Although I am a little confused as the couple you lived with in South Heath said that you came back to the house just after eleven o'clock in the evening, packed your bags and left for the station.'

'Oh right. Must be just after then, then,' Owen said.

'That wouldn't quite be right, though, would it? Because I've also seen the reports which say that Elliot Carr died between eleven thirty and eleven forty-five that night. That means that when you left the Manor Hotel, Elliot Carr was still alive. So why did you really leave?'

Hardwick sat and observed Owen as he absorbed the impact of this bombshell.

'I just had to go, all right?' he said. Hardwick said nothing, but just raised his eyebrow. 'Look, if you must know, I didn't resign. I was asked to leave.'

'By whom?'

'By Barbara. She was technically my boss, I suppose. I hadn't been happy there for ages, she wasn't happy with me either so it was a kinda mutual thing. All right? That's why I was upset and that's why I couldn't stay in South Heath and had to come back to Brighton. You do believe me, don't you?'

'Strangely enough, I do,' said Hardwick.

36

Scarlett Carr swallowed hard as she sat in the waiting room at the doctor's surgery. She didn't want to seem suspicious by constantly asking the lady on reception if the appointment could be kept completely confidential, but she had to be sure.

The receptionist saying 'Yes, appointments are generally confidential' hadn't exactly been overly helpful, as Scarlett couldn't exactly reply with 'Well, I mean if the police come sniffing around you won't give them my medical records, will you?'

She took a sharp intake of breath as the electronic sign bleeped and her name flashed up, telling her to go to consultation room 3. Picking up her handbag from the seat next to her, she jumped up and did as the sign instructed.

The smile of the doctor did nothing to put her at ease as she closed the door of consultation room 3 and sat down on the cream-coloured chair.

'So, what can I do for you today?' the doctor asked, not letting his grin slip.

'I... Uh...' *Come on, out with it*, Scarlett willed herself. She took a deep breath. 'I'm pregnant. I've done a few tests, different brands, and it's a definite. It'll be my first child so I'm not quite sure what to do next.'

'I see,' the doctor said, leaning back in his chair. 'Have you thought about what you want to do?'

'What do you mean?'

'Well, do you intend to keep the baby?'

'God, yes!' Scarlett said, a little too sharply. 'I'd never even consider... God, no. Yes, I want to keep it.'

'That's fine. I just needed to ask. Generally we tend to refer you on to the hospital in Shafford for your prenatal scans. They'll be regular throughout the pregnancy, just to keep an eye on the baby and make sure everything's all right. Do you know how far gone you are?'

'I'm not sure. About a month and a half, I think. Maybe two months.'

'No problem. We can get a better idea on the first scan, or I can arrange for a more in-depth pregnancy test if you'd like. That'll give us a much clearer indication of the date of conception. Would you like that?'

Scarlett froze. She knew this was something she was going to have to face, but she didn't quite know how. Deep down, she knew what the result would be. She knew who the father was. Based on the dates, it could only be one person.

'Uh, possibly. I'd need to have a think. It's all a bit sudden.'

'I totally understand. I've got a couple of leaflets here which might help,' the doctor replied, thumbing through a ring binder. 'Have you discussed the pregnancy with the father?' he asked, without looking up at her. *Might as well be honest for once in your life*, Scarlett told herself before taking a deep breath.

'Yes. Yes I have.'

37

Hardwick felt like he was going round and round in circles. Most of the circles, though, were broken, never quite meeting up where they were expected to. There seemed to be nothing to connect the two deaths and not even a motive for that of Kimberly Gray. He was reminded of the maxim of all great detectives, coined by the very greatest himself: *Once you eliminate the impossible, whatever remains, no matter how improbable, must be the truth.*

The sensible theory would be that both were suicides. That seemed like the logical and most possible solution in many ways, but it still didn't quite sit right with Hardwick. All he had to go on was the fact that both suicides were so close together time-wise and were almost identical in their execution. That, then, opened up the theory of Kimberly Gray's death being a copycat suicide. But why? She had no reason to want to end her life and by all accounts was in good spirits on the night of her death.

That also implied that Elliot Carr's death had been a suicide, which Hardwick was convinced was not the case. There seemed to be two distinct motives there: financial difficulties (granted, also a motive for suicide) and the relationship his wife was having with Kevin McGready, which again could also be construed as a reason for killing himself. It just didn't seem to fit in with what he knew of Elliot Carr as a person from speaking to friends and relatives, though. But if he had been murdered, that meant the same person must have killed Kimberly Gray, didn't it?

Unless, of course, Elliot Carr had been killed by someone else, Kimberly Gray had read about it as it had been reported as a suicide and had decided to copy it. But the same question came back: *why?*

He knew the answer lay right at the beginning and that there was no point in trying to fill in missing links halfway through the narrative. On the way back from Brighton, his train stopped at a number of stations between London and South Heath. One such station was Bellingham, so Hardwick once again found himself knocking on the door of Scarlett Carr's house, armed with fresh information on the financial difficulties her and Elliot had been facing.

Scarlett looked the picture of perfection as usual as she answered the door to her home and welcomed Hardwick in. Once he was settled in the living room with a cup of tea in his hand, he got straight to the point, as was his wont.

'Mrs Carr, can I ask: did you know anything about a large amount of credit card debt in yours and your husband's name?'

Scarlett shifted noticeable in her seat. 'I knew we had some debt, yes. Doesn't everyone?'

'That all depends on what you mean by "some", doesn't it?' Hardwick asked, before taking a sip of his tea, not once taking his eyes off of Scarlett Carr.

'Well, I don't know the exact amount. Elliot was always the one who took control of the financial stuff.'

'Yes, but Elliot's not here any more, is he? Surely you'll have to take over all of that now, and presumably you've got in contact with your creditors and discussed everything? Unless, of course, Kevin McGready is going to be the one who looks after the finances now.'

'And what do you mean by that exactly?' Scarlett asked, a sudden flash of anger in her eyes.

Hardwick smiled amiably. 'Nothing at all. Just that you said you weren't very good with financial things and I thought that as you were in a relationship with Mr McGready and now your husband is off the scene, perhaps he might be the one to take on that responsibility for you.'

Scarlett sat silently for a few moments, not breaking eye contact with Hardwick. He could see exactly what was going through her mind: she was trying to work out whether he was insinuating something or just asking innocent questions. Either way, she had to play the innocent to avoid incriminating herself by getting too defensive.

'I doubt it. I'll have to get on top of it all myself. I think I'd rather get the funeral and everything out of the way first, though.'

'It'll be quite difficult to manage the debts and pay them all back, though, won't it? Without a job, I mean.'

'I don't know,' Scarlett replied. 'I haven't looked at the details yet.'

'I have,' Hardwick said, pulling a scrap of paper from his inside jacket pocket. '£36,340 on a credit card, nearly forty thousand on car finance for the BMW and almost thirty thousand for the Range Rover.'

'Where did you get all this from?' Scarlett asked, looking visibly shocked.

'When someone dies in suspicious circumstances, it becomes a police matter, Mrs Carr. These sorts of things are investigated and looked at.' Hardwick was very careful to choose his words and not make out that he was a police officer.

'Suspicious circumstances?' Scarlett asked.

'Well, yes. Suicides by their very nature are suspicious circumstances as far as the police are concerned. It's an unexpected death. Why, what did you think I meant?' Hardwick asked innocently.

'Nothing,' Scarlett said, shifting again in her seat. 'I just wondered what you meant, that's all.'

Hardwick smiled and nodded. 'Can I ask, do you think Elliot would have killed himself to spite you? Perhaps he found out about your relationship with Kevin McGready and thought that he'd drop you in it at the same time.' He knew he was feeding her this theory rather than allowing her to dig her own holes, but he had his own very good reasons.

'I don't know. I doubt it. I don't think he was the type. And what do you mean drop me in it?' Scarlett asked.

'Well, by killing himself he would have not only escaped from his situation in terms of the debt and his wife being about to leave him, but he would have also invalidated his life insurance policy, ensuring that you were personally left liable for every penny of the debt upon his death.'

Hardwick watched Scarlett's face as her jaw fell. It seemed he had correctly predicted that she probably would not have worked that out for herself beforehand. 'I presume you didn't realise that already. Sorry to be the bearer of bad news,' he said, taking great pleasure in acting as sympathetically as he could. There was something — many things — about Scarlett Carr that he didn't like.

'No, it's fine. Not as if I haven't had enough shocks recently,' Scarlett said, trying to regain her composure. 'I'll have to sell the house. I can't stay here now anyway, not after... Well, not after all that's happened. It doesn't seem right.'

'Probably for the best,' Hardwick said. 'Would the equity in the house cover the debts, then? By my calculations there's over a hundred thousand pounds owing and I think I saw somewhere that your house was remortgaged fairly recently.'

Scarlett started blinking rapidly. She was clearly not a woman who was particularly good at hiding her thoughts or emotions, but on the same measure she wasn't someone who would easily give in or back down.

'There'll be something we can do. There has to be. Like I said, I haven't had time to look at all the details yet.'

Hardwick heard her voice break slightly on the last couple of words and chose not to say anything, instead letting her process her own thoughts.

'Oh god,' she finally said, as the tears started to roll down her cheeks and her shoulders began to tremble. 'What am I going to do?'

Hardwick was saved from having to comfort her by the sound of a key turning in the lock and the front door creaking open. A couple of seconds later it closed and the sound of footsteps coming towards the living room got louder and louder as Kevin McGready entered the room.

'Oh. Didn't know you had visitors,' he said to Scarlett.

'Mr McGready, what a pleasure it is,' Hardwick said. 'I see you've got your own key. That's handy.'

'What do you mean by that?'

'Nothing at all. Like I said, it's handy. You can pop round and see how Scarlett's getting on.'

'Right. And what are you doing here in the first place?' Kevin asked. 'I thought I told your mate not to bother coming round again.'

'You did. You told him not to go to your flat. You didn't tell me not to come to Scarlett's house.'

'Are you trying to be funny with me mate?' Kevin said loudly as Scarlett jumped up and grabbed his arm.

'Kevin, don't! Leave it. He just came to ask me some questions, that's all. He knows. All right?'

'Knows what?'

'About the financial stuff. Just leave it, all right?'

'I was going to say, Mrs Carr, that there's been a second death at the Manor Hotel. I know it seems very odd to ask it, but I have to do so as a matter of course because you were both connected to Elliot Carr. Where were you on Friday night?'

'What, so now you think I not only bumped off Elliot but that I'm a serial killer as well. Is that it?' Kevin said.

'Not at all. We just need to ask everyone.'

'I was at home. So was Scarlett. Happy now?'

'Thank you,' Hardwick said. 'It's just procedure.'

'Procedure?' Kevin asked. 'For who? The police?'

Hardwick could see where this was going. He pulled his notepad out of one of his jacket pockets and produced a pen from the other.

'If you could just jot that down for me, Mr McGready, then I promise I'll be able to leave you be.'

'Jot what down?'

'Just write "Scarlett Carr and I were both in our respective houses on the night of the second suicide, signed Kevin McGready." That should do.'

'Then you'll leave us alone?'

'Of course. If you have nothing to hide.'

Kevin McGready stared at Hardwick for a few moments before grinding his teeth, picking up the pen and beginning to write.

Once he'd finished, Hardwick put the pen back in his pocket, glanced at the paper and smiled.

'Thank you, Mr McGready. That'll be all for now.'

38

The Manor Hotel felt like a strange kind of home to Rosie Blackburn. It wasn't her actual home, but then again she wasn't sure what was. The house she owned and lived in wasn't far away at all, but it could hardly feel like home seeing as she'd only just moved in. She didn't quite have the same attachment to her previous home as most people would after a number of years, either.

Sure, the old house *had* been home, but that sense of security and belonging had been cruelly torn from her four years ago and it hadn't come back since. That feeling that something was missing was a feeling that she would never be able to shake. Nowhere would ever feel like home again. The Manor Hotel was the closest she'd ever come, though.

She'd come here every year on this day for the past four years and had felt both comfortable and safe, knowing that this was her tradition. This was her place on this day of the year. Every other day of the year had got progressively easier as time had gone by. The pain had never gone away, but it had dulled, become numb. This one particular day never got any easier, though. That was why she came to the Manor Hotel to be on her own and to both escape and be with her memories, short as they were.

Some of the coping mechanisms were working well. Her counsellor had convinced her to try meditation and relaxation therapies, which'd had some benefits. The concept of talking to people — people she didn't know — about what had happened was something she had been unable to do up until now. But somehow the fog was lifting slightly. She'd told herself that if the subject came up in conversation she'd talk about what had happened four years ago.

She knew it wouldn't be easy. She knew she'd probably break down in floods of tears. It would be the first time she had properly addressed the situation with another person, but it had to be done.

Once she'd checked in, Rosie hauled her overnight bag over her shoulder and made her way up the staircase to her room. The hotel seemed quieter than usual, which was hardly a surprise considering the stories in the news about the two suicides recently. That didn't bother her, though. She'd almost become desensitised to death.

In her room, she took her change of clothes out of her overnight bag and laid them on the bed. In the bottom of her bag, next to her toiletries holder, was a small framed photograph. She brought it here every year and knew she had to be close to it. It was a permanent reminder of what she'd been through, but it was also a huge comfort.

She should have been at home tidying up paper plates sodden in jelly and ice cream and waving off the last of the tired toddlers as their mothers came to collect them but it was not to be. Instead, she was here at the Manor Hotel, as she was every year, escaping from the absence of the family life she should have had.

She looked at herself in the small gilt-edged mirror over the dressing table, gazing deep into her own eyes. She saw nothing. Rosie had never been one for wearing lots of make-up, but she dabbed some powder and blusher on her cheeks and topped up her lipstick before changing into her spare clothes and making her way downstairs to the lounge room, locking the hotel room door behind her.

39

The evening had gone relatively smoothly for Kit Daniels. He and Becky had watched two films and got through two bottles of wine, and all without her having nagged him about getting their own place together.

It was the evenings in with Becky which really got to him as she'd always make some comment about how nice it would be if they could do this every night in a place of their own. How lovely it would be not to have to part ways afterwards. How it would make them feel like a *real couple*.

It wasn't that Kit didn't want to commit or that he didn't agree with her. Far from it. He just felt impotent and helpless as to what he could do about it. Things would change, though. He knew that much.

The pattern was all too predictable. As the credits rolled on the second film, Becky yawned and drained her glass of wine. Honestly, sometimes it was like going out with a robot and living through Groundhog Day at the same time. He braced himself for what he knew was coming, the red wine sloshing about in his head.

'I meant to ask, how's that story going at work?' Becky said innocently, trying to pretend it was just a passing thought as she pulled the fluffy jumper over her head.

'We're getting there,' Kit replied. 'Do you want me to walk you back?'

'Only if you don't mind. You're such a sweetie. You know, I can't wait until I can spend every evening with you.'

Kit forced a smile and put on his shoes and jacket.

They were barely a hundred yards down the road before Becky broached the subject yet again. 'How close are we to doing it, Kit?' she asked, looking up at him inquisitively as she held his hand a little tighter.

'To doing what?' he replied, knowing full well what she meant.

'To getting our own place.'

'I'm doing my best, Becky. You don't have to keep bugging me about it, all right?'

'Because I was thinking, we could start looking at places and getting a feel for what we like. Perhaps speak to a mortgage advisor and see what we'd need to save and what sort of money they'd give us. Just so we know where we stand. Don't you think?'

Kit could feel the blood thumping at his temples as he tried to control his anger.

'For Christ's sake, can't you just give it a bloody rest?' he barked as they walked past the communal garage block which joined the two estates.

'But it's important to me, Kit. I thought it was to you, too. Look, if you don't want to then at least just have the decency to tell me.'

Before Becky could even wait for a reply, she found herself pinned against the nearest garage door, her back having hit the sheet metal with an oddly satisfying *thwump*. She could hear only the echoing of the metallic impact and the blood pulsing in her ears as she stared into Kit's wild eyes, his hand constricted round her throat.

'For once in your bloody life, will you just shut up!' he yelled, the warm alcoholic fumes hitting her face like a tsunami.

'Kit, you're hurting me,' she squeaked as she saw the life return to his eyes. Kit's grip relaxed and he took a step back as Becky's hand shot to her throat. She found no words as she just stared at him, watching him pace back and forth across the concrete, rubbing his head.

'I can't handle this pressure, Becky. I'm sorry. I didn't mean it. I just... Look, I don't know. It's just building up. Believe me, I'm doing everything I can to make you happy but you're making it so bloody impossible for me.'

Becky remained impassive, staring at him.

'Becky? Please. I didn't mean to hurt you,' he said, gripping her forearms and looking into her eyes, seeing her visibly flinch as he did so. 'I don't know what happens. It's just been building up. I'm so sorry. I've just been under so much pressure and this really isn't helping. Look, I'm going to sort this out, all right? Please just stop asking me about it. I've got something in the pipeline right as we speak and when it breaks it's going to set us up for life. All right?'

Becky swallowed and nodded, not quite sure exactly what she was agreeing to.

WEDNESDAY 25TH MARCH

40

Ellis Flint was thoroughly engrossed in the old black and white western on TV, but answered his ringing phone almost immediately, as he usually did.

'Ellis? Hardwick here. Listen, I'm in a phone box on my way to speak to Detective Inspector Warner, so I can't chat for long. I just wanted to keep you updated. Something very strange happened on Monday morning. I received a death threat.'

'What? Are you serious?' Ellis said, those being the first words he'd managed to squeeze in since pressing the "answer" button on his phone.

'Absolutely. But I wouldn't worry. I know who it was from.'

'Who?'

'Kevin McGready. Fortunately, he turned up while I was at Scarlett Carr's house. I managed to get him to write down his alibi for the night Kimberly Gray died.'

'What? You don't honestly think he killed Kimberly Gray, do you, Kempston?' Ellis asked.

'Oh no, not in the slightest. I only wanted his alibi written down so I could compare his writing to the note I received. He tried to obscure the handwriting, but not enough. Besides which, it was a little grammatical peculiarity which gave him away. He has a dreadful habit of spelling "our" a-r-e. That gave him away somewhat.'

'Right. So what are you going to do about it?'

'Nothing. There's nothing to do and no point in doing anything. As I said, I don't really think he's a credible suspect so I shan't be poking around in his business, as he sees it.'

'But how can you say he's not a suspect, Kempston? He had a damn good reason to want Elliot Carr dead. And we still don't know where he was on the night Elliot Carr died.'

'He wasn't at the Manor Hotel, that much is certain. I've seen the CCTV footage of people coming and going from the front entrance — the only entrance — on the night he died. Kevin McGready isn't on it.'

'Well who is? Surely the killer must be on the CCTV,' Ellis said excitedly.

'You'd imagine so, yes.'

'So why don't you just get their names and addresses off the hotel and we can go and speak to them all? We've got a closed circle of suspects, Kempston.'

'It's not quite that simple, Ellis,' Kempston said, sighing as he pushed another pound coin into the payphone. 'I looked at the CCTV footage from the night Kimberly Gray died, too. Far fewer guests that night after the news of Elliot Carr's death beforehand, and none of them were there on both nights. The only people who were there on both nights were staff members, as you'd expect.'

'Is there another way into the hotel?'

'Not that I know of. I mean, of course there are french windows and fire exits and what have you, which I suppose is what I'd use if I was going to break into a hotel and kill someone. The CCTV doesn't cover them all, though. Only the ones which can be opened from the outside.'

'So if someone went in through an already open door which only opened from the inside, they could get in without being seen?'

'That's about the long and short of it, yes. And as the hotel only has a few rooms, CCTV on the floors is very limited.'

'Right. So what do we do now?'

'As I see it, if the deaths are connected and both Elliot Carr and Kimberly Gray were murdered, then it's very difficult to see how the same person could've killed them both. The only people there on both nights were the members of hotel staff and none of them even knew Elliot and Kimberly, let alone had a reason to kill them, knowing they'd become the prime suspects if they did.'

'Except for Owen Bartlett, who did a runner.'

'Indeed. But he wasn't in the area when the second death occurred. Which means we'd then be looking at two separate killers. Why would they both kill in exactly the same way in exactly the same place? They'd have to be connected in some way. In cahoots, perhaps. Failing that, the third possibility is the one that I somehow feel least happy with. That they were both suicides and that Kimberly Gray's was a copycat suicide. It just doesn't ring true, though. It doesn't feel right.' A sudden moment of clarity hit Hardwick. 'Or maybe there's no link at all. Maybe that's just it. Maybe the victims weren't the target.'

'How can they not be the target?' Ellis asked.

'Maybe the victims were just collateral. Maybe someone had a grudge against the hotel.'

'Owen Bartlett?'

'Perhaps. Or maybe someone had a grudge against a particular person and wanted to set them up for murder.'

'So why make it look like suicide?' Ellis asked.

'That's what I'm not quite sure of at the moment.'

Ellis was silent for a few moments. 'Kempston, do you ever think that perhaps for once your feeling might be wrong?'

Hardwick swallowed hard before speaking. 'No, Ellis. I don't.'

41

'You'd better have something good for me, Hardwick. And I mean bloody good,' Detective Inspector Rob Warner said as Hardwick entered his hallway.

Hardwick knew he didn't have something good, other than his hunch. DI Rob Warner was not a man who worked from hunches, but he was occasionally vulnerable to being gradually worn down over time until he gave up and acquiesced.

'Yes and no,' Hardwick said. 'I've spoken to Kimberly Gray's parents and friends.'

'You've done what?' Warner croaked, by now resigned to Hardwick's whims and insistence.

'It's not a crime, is it?' Hardwick asked innocently.

'That all depends, doesn't it? Did you go around telling them you were a police officer again?'

'I never once claimed to be a police officer, no. I never

have. If people choose to believe that, it's not for me to disabuse them of the notion.'

'Don't get clever with me, Hardwick. What did they say?'

'They said that Kimberly wasn't the sort of person to kill herself. Quite the opposite, in fact. They said that she had been having the time of her life recently. Absolutely no indication that she would do anything like that.'

'Well yes, that's often the case,' Warner said, leaning back on his reclining chair in a manner which suggested a nonchalant confidence over Hardwick. 'You never know what people are going through privately. That doesn't mean she wasn't mentally ill, though, does it?'

'No, but it does make it rather unlikely,' Hardwick said. 'I also spoke to Owen Bartlett.'

'Who?'

'The employee at the Manor Hotel who disappeared on the night Elliot Carr died. He went back to his mother's house in Brighton.'

'Right,' Warner said. 'I see.' Hardwick could see that this piece of information hadn't been relayed to Warner until now. For the first time, he felt that he finally had the upper hand.

'Something wasn't quite right about him. He was definitely hiding something. I can tell you that much. But it wasn't what I'd expected, I must be honest. First of all he told me that he hadn't enjoyed working at the Manor Hotel for a long time and that finding out Elliot Carr had died had tipped him over the edge and he'd left. Fairly plausible, I grant you. But I'd already asked the people he was living with in South Heath, and they told me he'd come back just after eleven o'clock that evening and then got on a train.' Hardwick stopped to let this information sink in.

Warner ruffled through a stack of papers, checking something. 'But Elliot Carr died about half an hour after that.'

'Indeed. So he hadn't even heard about Elliot Carr's death when he decided to leave, let alone be affected by it, because Elliot Carr was still alive at that point.'

'So why did he leave?' Warner asked.

'A disagreement with another member of staff, he says. He'd wanted to go for a while and the argument pushed him over the edge.'

'So why lie? That's a perfectly reasonable explanation in itself. Why throw the suicide of Elliot Carr into the mix? If he'd told you he wasn't even at the bloody hotel when Elliot Carr died, that's the story over. He's not a witness nor a suspect. So why did he lie?'

'That's what I want to know,' Hardwick said. 'And I can see that you do, too.'

Warner exhaled deeply. 'It does seem odd. Listen, I agree that we need to look more closely at this. Perhaps. This Owen Bartlett bloke is hiding something, I agree, but that's not to say that it's linked with any sort of crime whatsoever. And definitely not bloody murder, before you say anything. See what you can find out, but if you dare suggest murder again, I'll make sure you're barred from ever entering the Manor Hotel again, is that clear?'

Hardwick let the awkwardness pass before speaking again. 'The toxicology reports on Elliot Carr and Kimberly Gray. Did they have anything other than alcohol in their systems?'

Warner sighed. 'If it'll shut you up, yes. Kimberly Gray had a half-digested cheeseburger and chips and Elliot Carr had a bag of pork scratchings. Happy?'

'I meant had they taken any drugs, or...'

'Or what?' Warner replied. 'Had they been poisoned? Simple answer is no. Absolutely no signs whatsoever.'

'I see,' Hardwick said. After a couple of moments of silence, he looked up and met Warner's eye. 'You know, Detective Inspector, whatever happened in the past in your life, you can't let it cloud your judgement.'

'I don't think I'm the one having my judgement clouded, Hardwick,' Warner replied.

'What happened with your mother was, no doubt, a terrible tragedy but you won't be able to find the answers you need in a completely unrelated case.'

Warner sat, stunned. Before he could reply, he was interrupted by the phone ringing on his coffee table. As he picked it up and answered it, Hardwick could see his face changing.

'Right. I see. The same one? Mmmhmmm. Right. Okay, I'll be right down.' Warner put the phone down and let out a huge sigh as he closed his eyes. 'Well, how's that for timing?' he said, looking at Hardwick. 'There's been another suicide at the Manor Hotel. And before you ask, yes: room thirteen, hanging, dressing gown cord. This pattern is starting to look a little too familiar for my liking.'

42

The scene at the Manor Hotel was very different when Hardwick and Warner arrived that evening. They'd had to meet Ellis at the end of the driveway, as the area around the hotel had been cordoned off by police tape. It was now clear to Hardwick that the local constabulary were treating the supposed suicides for what they were.

Warner had driven Hardwick to South Heath in complete silence. Warner himself had nothing to say as the constable on the phone said he'd give him all of the relevant information at the scene. Hardwick didn't push Warner for conversation and instead preferred to sit in silence, hoping the Detective Inspector would be stewing on his reluctance to have accepted Hardwick's theory of foul play earlier.

When the trio arrived at the front door of the Manor Hotel, Warner immediately spoke to a uniformed officer standing in reception.

'Who is it?' Warner asked.

'Woman called Rosie Blackburn. At least that's the name she signed in under, anyway. There's an officer in her hotel room going through her belongings. Should be able to confirm ID from that.'

'Right. And who found the body?'

'The receptionist, sir. A Mandy Slater. She's through in the lounge. A bit shaken, as you can imagine.'

Hardwick, Flint and Warner made their way through to the lounge amidst the murmuring and crackling of police radios and found Mandy Slater being comforted by Barbara, of not-working-the-coffee-machine fame.

'Miss Slater? DI Rob Warner, Tollinghill Police. This is Kempston Hardwick and Ellis Flint.'

'Yes, we've met,' Mandy replied, looking at Hardwick and Flint through the tears in her eyes.

'Oh, you have, have you?' Warner replied, looking at Hardwick. 'Why am I not surprised. Sorry to intrude at such an upsetting time, but it was you who found the body, yes?'

'Yes,' she replied, tears rolling down her cheeks as she recalled the moment. 'She was just hanging there... Like a rag doll... Oh Jesus Christ, it was horrible!'

'Mandy, language. I know you're upset, dear,' Barbara said, rubbing her hand on Mandy's upper back.

'And might I ask why you'd gone up to room thirteen?' Warner asked, trying to sound as sensitive and understanding as possible.

'Ah. That would be me,' Barbara replied. 'Mandy was

showing some guests to their room and I asked her to pop up and grab a couple of fresh tea towels for the bar on her way back.'

'And who called the police?'

'I did,' Mandy replied. 'It was just instinct. There's an emergency phone on the top floor and I just called 999 straight away. The officers who came were the same two who came last time, when... You know...' Mandy rested her head on Barbara's shoulder and continued sobbing.

'Yes, we know. We can see you're very upset, Miss Slater. We'll come back a little later. Please don't go anywhere without speaking to me first, though, as we need to make sure we know where everyone is.'

As Warner, Hardwick and Flint ascended the stairs to the top floor, Warner stopped at the first floor landing and addressed Hardwick and Flint.

'Now listen. This is a crime scene as far as I'm concerned, all right? That's what you wanted to hear, and that's what you've got. But it's my backside that's on the line here so don't go touching anything, okay? You stand in the doorway and look and you let me know straight away if you spot any of your odd little patterns or whatever, but that's it. I'm only letting you that far because you've helped me out in the past.'

'Understood, Detective Inspector,' Hardwick said in his most serious voice.

Ellis Flint just nodded vigorously, like a schoolchild

being given the opportunity to leave school to run an errand for a teacher.

Another young police officer was standing in the doorway to room thirteen as they reached the top floor. The rafters were exposed right across this floor of the house, and the headspace was limited, especially closer to the walls. The area would be barely useable as loft space, so it didn't surprise Hardwick or Flint that the hotel chose to use it as storage and that it had gone unnoticed for so many years before that.

Ducking to walk under the door, Hardwick stood just inside the room and took in what he could see. Warner nodded at one of the forensics officers inside the room to signal that they could bring the body down and lay it on the floor. A chair lay on its side about six feet from where the woman's body had been hanging.

'Has anyone moved this chair?' Warner asked.

'No, sir,' one of the forensics officers replied. 'We've got photographs of it in situ. Everything was photographed as per usual.'

'Right. Have it looked at closely. I specifically want to know if it's consistent with having been kicked away by the deceased. Have them look at the dressing gown cord, too.'

'I was going to mention that, actually,' the forensics officer said. 'It's a double granny knot at both ends, tied tight around the neck, same as the other two. Not technically a noose. Would've been a slow, painful death, to be honest. Not as quick as a slip knot, especially not with the short drop here.'

'Why were the dressing gowns and cords still stored in here?' Hardwick asked. 'Surely if two people had already died in this room and in that manner in the space of eight days they'd keep them elsewhere.'

'Like where?' Warner said. 'This is the bloody store-room, Hardwick. It's where stuff's stored. It's under lock and key. What else do you want?' Hardwick didn't reply. 'How long would it have taken?' Warner asked the forensics officer.

'Impossible to say. Depends on the weight of the person, their physical state, not to mention the specific measurements. We can have a better idea once we've looked more closely.'

Warner turned round to look at Hardwick. Hardwick knew Warner was thinking exactly the same thing as him: if the death had taken anywhere around the half an hour mark, it was entirely possible that Owen Bartlett could have hanged Elliot Carr before leaving the Manor Hotel, with Elliot Carr finally dying painfully and agonisingly more than half an hour later. But why would he risk that? Why risk someone entering the room in the meantime and finding Elliot Carr still alive, able to identify his assailant? Besides which, Owen Bartlett had been in Brighton when Kimberly Gray and Rosie Blackburn had died, so couldn't have been involved with their deaths. Something didn't add up.

The officer stood in the doorway answered his crack-ling radio before speaking to Warner.

'You're wanted downstairs, sir, in the deceased's room.'

. . .

When Hardwick, Flint and Warner got down to the room Rosie Blackburn had been staying in, they found a small team of police officers going through her personal effects and bagging any items of interest. They had confirmed her identity and were trying to piece together what had gone on in the build up to her death.

'We've managed to get in touch with her husband, sir,' one of the officers said. 'She was sensible enough to have him listed as her ICE contact in her phone, which she left in her room.'

Warner nodded. He considered it good advice to ensure that the next of kin's name in people's mobile phones should be marked *ICE*, for In Case of Emergency. That way, the police's job was made much easier in terms of getting in touch with someone's next of kin should something happen to them.

'She was fairly local, actually,' the officer added. 'They live in Tollinghill. The husband was saying she comes to stay here once a year on the same night every year. It's the anniversary of the day her newborn child died, so she has to get away.'

'Did the husband not come too?' Warner asked.

'No, apparently she always said it was easier on her own. Didn't want the reminders. Just needed to be away from home for the night.'

'Bit odd that, isn't it?' Warner said, looking at Hardwick. Hardwick was not one for necessarily always understanding human emotion, but even he was a little taken aback by Warner's remarks.

'I think it might be best if we spoke to Rosie Blackburn's husband, don't you?' Hardwick said.

'Sorry, we?' Warner asked, shoving his hands in his pockets and turning to face Hardwick.

'Well I don't think we can afford any more missed opportunities, can we, Detective Inspector?'

43

With Hardwick and Warner having gone to speak to the husband of Rosie Blackburn, Ellis had been left at home to pursue his own suspicions as to what could be behind the deaths.

Hardwick still wouldn't waver from his main theory that all three had been murdered, but Ellis was less convinced. He was now moving away from the theory that there was some sort of paranormal explanation and was looking for a credible theory to put forward.

Deep down, though, Ellis knew that the deaths of Elliot Carr, Kimberly Gray and Rosie Blackburn probably were the work of a killer. He also knew that he absolutely did not want to accept that theory. Finding a killer is difficult enough anyway, but finding someone who kills so seemingly randomly and indiscriminately would be almost impossible.

So it was with sheer hope and optimism that he sat

down in the coffee shop with Dr Alan Harding, who he'd contacted in order to discuss the prevalence of copycat suicides and mass hysteria. He'd done a bit of research on the subject and wanted to find out more from the man who claimed to be one of the leading experts on the subject.

'Your email mentioned something about mass hysteria?' Dr Harding prompted, after ten or fifteen minutes of Ellis talking about the problems he'd been having with his combi boiler.

'Ah, yes. I'm not sure if you've seen in the papers the stuff about the deaths at the Manor Hotel in South Heath...' Ellis left the sentence dangling.

'I recall seeing something, yes. Why?'

'Well, the police aren't swerving from their line that all three were suicides. I mean, they definitely looked like suicides. And in a way I guess I'd like to think they were, if you see what I mean.'

'Compared to the alternative?' Dr Harding said.

'Indeed. Now, I've read a little bit about copycat suicides and things, but it doesn't quite seem to ring true with what's happening here. These people on the whole didn't seem like they would take their own lives. Well, one certainly didn't. The other two are debatable.'

'Why's that?' the doctor asked.

'One of them had probably just found out his wife was leaving him after putting him in an enormous amount of debt and the other was grieving over a child who died at birth and had just been through a stressful house move,' Ellis explained.

'I see. And the other?'

'Nothing at all, it seems. Quite the opposite actually. She had just passed her driving test, just turned eighteen and just been to see a pop concert she'd been desperate to go to.'

Dr Harding ran his fingers through his beard. 'And in what order did the deaths occur?'

'First one was Elliot Carr, the bloke who's wife was about to do a runner; second was Kimberly Gray, the eighteen-year-old; third was Rosie Blackburn, the woman who'd lost a baby.'

'Ah. I ask because if the second two had been aware of the previous suicides at the hotel, it's quite possible that under situations of extreme stress, some form of hysteria could have set in. It's incredibly easily done, actually. It could be a form of what we call anxiety hysteria, in which something like a smell or other sensory input can cause physical and psychological symptoms to manifest.'

'What about the paranormal?' Ellis asked, before noticing Dr Harding raise one eyebrow. 'I mean, there are stories about hauntings at the Manor Hotel. I don't believe them myself, of course not, but would that same theory apply? That if all three had heard about the ghost stories, they might have been more open to these sensory inputs which might have caused them to... Well, go doolally.'

'"Trigger a psychosomatic response" is what we'd say, but yes, it's perfectly possible. In fact, there's something called psychomotor agitation, which is actually quite common amongst ghost hunters and paranormal investigators. The pent-up anxiety which builds up over time manifests itself physically. They're also — often more dangerously — prone to demopathic hysteria, where they believe that someone or something has followed them home from a ghost hunt and they start to believe that these are real people haunting them.'

'Could that be it?' Ellis asked excitedly. 'That the three people had this sense that a spirit was personally haunting them and telling them to kill themselves?'

'It's possible, yes,' Dr Harding said. 'Let's just suppose for a moment that all three had heard of the ghost stories. Out of the tens of thousands of people who visit the Manor Hotel every year, three of them having heard a pretty well publicised ghost story isn't unusual. Our first chap, Carr, is under an enormous amount of stress as you say. He's also susceptible to demopathic hysteria or something similar. What's to say that this smorgasbord of stress and psychological anomalies didn't combine to manifest some sort of compulsion to suicide?'

Ellis nodded, pretending he'd understood every word the doctor said.

'Now, that first suicide was fairly well publicised in the press, yes? So the details of how it was done could potentially be read by anyone. Let's assume that Kimberly Gray reads one of these news reports and subconsciously retains that information. Which she will have done, if she'd read the reports. We subconsciously retain enormous amounts of information, particularly things which shock or inspire.

Now, you mention that she was under a great deal of stress too.'

'No, not at all,' Ellis said. 'She'd been having a great time.'

'Ah, I think we have different definitions of stress. It need not be negative. A big birthday, the huge event of finally being able to drive and the responsibilities that come with that, plus the potentially life-changing event — for her — of seeing her idol on stage that night. All positive things, you might think, but they are all big events and will all cause stress, whether positive or negative stress. It's important we don't differentiate as stress is stress in this instance. Something, then, could have compelled her to kill herself in the same manner.'

'And I suppose the same goes for Rosie Blackburn?' Ellis asked.

'Absolutely. She'd been under enormous amounts of negative stress, as you say. Losing a child is just the most horrific thing a person can go through, trust me,' Dr Harding said as his voice cracked slightly. 'And they say that moving house is one of the most stressful things a person can do in their life. Combine that with the possibility that she may well have been aware of the news reports about the two previous deaths — which were by then pretty much everywhere — and perhaps a latent or subconscious memory of hearing stories of hauntings at the Manor Hotel and you've got a potential psychological atom bomb.'

Ellis was immensely satisfied and yet still not. To know

that there was a perfectly viable psychological explanation behind this phenomenon was reassuring, yet something still didn't seem quite right. It all seemed rather too theoretical. *Yes, this* could *happen... Sometimes it's* possible *that... Theoretically speaking...*

Besides which, for Ellis Flint there was one huge, unshakeable factor which he could not ignore. Hardwick was convinced it was murder. And Hardwick was rarely mistaken.

44

DI Warner's ageing Volvo squealed as it pulled up on the kerb outside Rosie Blackburn's house. Hardwick noticed a man peering from behind the curtains, and it was this same man who had opened the front door by the time he and Warner had made their way halfway up the path, having dropped Ellis off at home. This was far too sensitive a situation for Hardwick to risk him putting his foot in it.

'Mr Blackburn?' Warner asked. He'd already made it quite clear to Hardwick in the car on the way over that it was he who would be doing the questioning as it was he who'd spent four months at Hendon for the privilege.

'You can call me Matthew,' the man said. Hardwick wouldn't, because he never did.

After being beckoned inside, Hardwick and Warner sat down on two dining room chairs which were on the floor in the living room amongst a mound of cardboard boxes.

'You'll have to excuse the mess. We only moved in a few days ago.'

'Oh, did you move far?' Warner asked.

'No, not really. We only lived round the corner before.'

'Well it can't be easy for you, especially not with... Well, you know,' Warner said.

'I know,' Matthew Blackburn replied. 'To be honest I think I'm just in shock. It's not sunk in. I just keep expecting her to walk in through the door any minute.'

'Is there anybody who can sit with you?' Warner asked. 'A family member or a friend?'

'I don't know. I mean, I called my parents and Rosie's and they're coming up, but they live down in Cornwall. That's where we're both from originally, you see. I just don't quite know what to do at the moment.' Matthew brought his hands to his mouth in a steeple and looked for a moment as though he might break down in tears.

'I know it's difficult and this is probably the last thing you want to talk about, but we need to get to the bottom of what happened. Did you suspect at any point that your wife might want to end her own life?'

Matthew stood silently for a couple of moments, clearly struggling with his emotions. 'Well yes, at some points. But not recently. Just after we lost our baby, she was absolutely devastated, of course she was. We both were. And on the anniversary each year she had to get away and escape. That was part of the reason for moving to a new house, so the memories weren't there.'

'Do you mind me asking what happened?' Warner asked.

'It was our daughter. She died during childbirth. Rosie blamed herself because she wanted a home birth and had refused a caesarian section. I mean, she didn't need to blame herself, of course. Home births are totally natural and safe and hospitals are always too quick to go for the c-section these days, aren't they? But there was no telling her. She blamed herself. The doctors and midwife said there was nothing she could have done and that it would have happened anyway, but she had this bee stuck in her bonnet that it was somehow her fault. I think that's why she felt she had to get away each year. Not far, as you know. Just away from the house and somewhere she felt comfortable. Just to forget who she was for twenty-four hours.'

'And she didn't want you there with her?' Warner asked.

'No, I did offer, but she said it would be the same in terms of being a reminder. She just wanted to forget for one day. That's not so bad, is it? Because believe me, not an hour goes past when I don't think about what happened to us and I know it was the same for Rosie, if not worse. We even gave her a name, you know? Isabelle. It's strange, but it feels like we really knew her. Even though she was technically never born, we still feel as if we had years with her before she was wrenched away. I know that probably sounds really odd, but it's true. I guess you just can't really explain it to someone who hasn't been there.'

Warner glanced at Hardwick, indicating that he could now speak if he wanted to. Hardwick could sense that Warner felt uncomfortable in the situation and that Hardwick would perhaps be better suited to knowing what to say.

'It sounds like a very stressful and upsetting time,' Hardwick finally said, choosing his words carefully.

'Yes, it never really goes away. I mean, of course you learn to deal with it and you have to let life carry on. But that doesn't mean you ever get over it. You never forget and it is always with you. But she would never have killed herself. Not at all,' Matthew said quickly and decisively. 'Absolutely not. Even when we were both at our lowest ebb, it was something she would have never done. She thought life was too valuable to be wasted like that. Even a painful life. That's why she was so distraught when we lost Isabelle. You know, she even lost a friend a couple of years earlier because she thought the friend was inconsiderate for having an abortion when she found out her unborn baby had Down's Syndrome. Rosie told her she should give the child a life regardless. They fell out over it and didn't speak after that.'

'Is it possible that the house move might have stirred up some emotions and unbalanced her? Especially at this time of year,' Hardwick said.

Matthew Blackburn's eyes seemed to well up before them as he seemed to consider that he might have had some influence on his wife's decision to take her own life.

'Oh God, I hadn't thought about that. But no, surely

not. I would have noticed. You don't think... Oh God.'

'No, Mr Blackburn,' Warner said. 'We don't. In fact, one of the reasons we're here is because we don't think Rosie took her own life at all. We think she might have been murdered.'

Although Warner had meant it to sound reassuring, it was clear to him and Hardwick that it had been the final nail in the coffin for Matthew, who deflated into a sobbing ball. It was a good fifteen minutes before the conversation could be brought back round to the subject of Rosie's untimely death.

'We have to ask this, I'm afraid,' Warner said as comfortingly as he could. 'Did your wife have any enemies? Anyone who might want to do her harm?'

'No, of course not!' Matthew replied, verging on the angry.

'What about the friend you told us about earlier? The one she fell out with over the abortion?' Hardwick suggested.

'No, absolutely not. They were both upset, but not in that sort of way. And anyway, they moved out to Australia a year later so you can forget all about that.'

Before Hardwick or Warner could open their mouths to ask another question, they were interrupted by the ringing of the doorbell. Matthew stood up and went to answer the door as Hardwick and Warner looked at each other without saying a word. A few seconds later, Matthew returned with a very upset-looking man and woman in their sixties.

'This is Sue and Pete, Rosie's parents,' Matthew said. 'Would you mind leaving us to have some time on our own? Please?'

'Yes, of course,' Warner said, getting in before Hardwick did. Although Warner knew he was not the most tactful of men, he was quite sure Hardwick would go one further if he were allowed to stay in a room with three grieving people. 'We will need to speak to you further, though. Perhaps you could make an appointment to come in and see me. Or I could come back to see you if you'd feel more comfortable chatting in your own home.'

Matthew Blackburn nodded and showed Warner and Hardwick out.

'What did you make of him?' Warner asked Hardwick as they made their way back to the car. 'I'm not sure. He seemed genuine enough to me, but then again that doesn't always mean a lot in my experience. What I would say, though, is next time you speak to him try and make sure it's not at his house. Either neutral territory or get him in to see you. That way, he might act differently and we might see a different side to him.'

'Is it not usually at home that people let their guards down?' Warner asked. 'Because if you're about to tell me that everything I've learnt on the force is crap again, Hardwick, I—'

'No no no, not at all, Detective Inspector,' Hardwick said, interrupting Warner mid-flow. 'But I think it's worth a try. Don't you?'

THURSDAY 26TH MARCH

45

DI Rob Warner blew across the rim of the plastic coffee cup as he read the front page of the Tollinghill Echo. The headline read:

LOCAL HOTEL IN SUICIDE SCANDAL: PARA-NORMAL INVESTIGATORS CALLED IN AFTER SECOND DEATH AS POSSIBLE SUICIDE CULT PROBED

Warner closed his eyes and shook his head, then looked at the byline. Of course. Kit Daniels. It had to be Kit Daniels. The shock jock of the local newspaper, intent on trying to get the juiciest possible stories to make a name for himself. He thanked his lucky stars that at least the paper hadn't yet got wind of the third death. If and when they did, that's when the proverbial would really hit the fan.

The newspaper's entire ethos was built around trying to publish sensationalist stories which they could then sell up to the nationals. With advertising revenues at an all time low — particularly in tatty rags such as the Echo — local newspapers had to resort to desperate tactics to generate income. The Tollinghill Echo was amongst the worst offenders and Kit Daniels was the most notorious amongst the Echo's journalists.

At least he's spelt everything correctly this time, Warner thought as he skimmed through the article. Before now, when Kit Daniels had been the first to break stories, Warner had wondered how on earth he'd got the information. He no longer bothered wasting his time thinking about it, as it was always the case. He was sure Daniels had a network of people on the ground, listening carefully in pubs and shops and passing up information from the grapevine in exchange for a small bung here and there.

Although Kit Daniels was known for not respecting the police and its investigations, even he could not deny that he needed to obey the law, even if he was prone to pushing it to its extremes. It was about time Warner put in a call.

He picked up the phone and dialled the number for Kit Daniels's direct line. The phone rang twice before it was picked up.

'Tollinghill Echo, Kit Daniels speaking.'

'Christopher, hello,' Warner said.

'Ah, Mr Warner. What a pleasure,' Kit said, knowing that the only person who referred to him by his full name was Tollinghill's local Detective Inspector.

'It might be for you, Daniels, but it's not for me. I've just seen your front page.'

'So have thousands, Detective Inspector. Good, isn't it? You should see the online version. The comments section has gone bananas. All sorts of nutcases out there. We've had everything from satanic cults to government brainwashing by the Illuminati so far, and it's only been live two hours.'

'And you think that sort of sensationalism is clever, do you?' Warner asked.

'Got to get people talking, haven't we? That's our job, after all. Just reporting the news. That's how it is. Keep you lot on your toes for starters.'

'We don't need keeping on our toes,' Warner replied. 'We're investigating two deaths here and the last thing we need is you sticking your oar in and stirring up a load of conspiracy theories.'

'Well what are your theories, Detective Inspector? Do you have any? I'm guessing not. What's wrong with a little outside help, in that case? I mean, you're not averse to using people from outside the police force to help you with investigations, are you?'

Warner knew damn well what Kit Daniels was referring to. He'd made remarks about Hardwick's involvement in investigations in the past, but he now had a feeling that he knew Hardwick was floating around the Manor Hotel situation, too.

'And anyway,' Kit Daniels continued. 'Are you actually investigating? Because the last I heard, you were treating the deaths as suicide. No investigation required, surely?'

'You know what I mean, Daniels,' Warner said. 'The gist of it is that it's nothing to do with you or your bird-brained readers. How much clearer do I have to make myself? I want you to stop reporting on this, pull the story from your online outlets and keep it out of your papers from now on. If — *if* — there is some sort of suicide cult going on, the last thing we want is new people joining in. All right?'

There was a short silence before Kit Daniels replied. 'We have a duty to report the news, Detective Inspector.'

Warner sighed. 'Do you want blood on your hands? Because if you continue along this path, that's what you'll get.'

46

The smell of black coffee assaulted Ellis Flint's nostrils as he sauntered into Hardwick's kitchen and headed straight for the pot of black liquid.

'Would you like a coffee, Ellis?' Hardwick asked sarcastically.

'Not to worry. I'm already doing it,' Ellis replied. 'Hope you've made it nice and strong. I'm having real trouble waking up at the moment. I must be getting ten hours of sleep a night. It's madness.'

Hardwick raised one eyebrow. 'Yes, well I've probably had about a tenth of that. And I'm not the one who goes to bed with eight mugs of coffee and thirty teaspoons of sugar sloshing about my bloodstream either.'

'Maybe you should give it a go. Works for me.'

'I think I'll pass, thank you, Ellis.'

Once he had made sure his coffee was sweeter than a pile of kittens in a Haribo factory, Ellis sat down at the kitchen table. It was then that he saw the wall covered in photographs, maps and scribbled notes.

There were maps of South Heath with the Manor Hotel marked and, Ellis was surprised to see, the locations of mobile phone masts which he'd researched earlier.

Hardwick noticed that Ellis was looking at the map. 'Just to make sure we've got all the information, Ellis. Before you start thinking I've fallen in for your daft theories. We have to eliminate all other possibilities.'

'Right. I believe you. Thousands wouldn't. Christ, where did you get all these photos of people from?' Ellis said, pointing to the pictures of Kimberly Gray, Elliot and Scarlett Carr, their friends and family and staff members at the Manor Hotel. There were arrows and lines connecting some of them, showing their relationships.

'Facebook, mostly. A couple of them I had to take myself.'

'And who's that one?' Ellis said, pointing to the picture of a pasty-looking young man with dark floppy hair.

'That's Owen Bartlett, Ellis,' Hardwick replied patronisingly. 'You went to Brighton to interview him.'

'No it isn't. Owen Bartlett has short, blonde hair. Very short. Shaved, I'd say.'

'Ellis, I took that photo of him myself when I went to speak to him the other day. He can't have just grown hair in the space of a couple of days.'

'Well that's not the bloke I talked to. I can absolutely guarantee that,' Ellis said, jabbing his finger at the photograph before taking a large swig of his coffee as if this was no big issue at all.

Hardwick stared at the photograph and blinked three times. 'You know what this means, don't you, Ellis? Only one of us spoke to Owen Bartlett. The other one was an imposter. And we've no way of knowing which one.'

47

DI Warner bowed his head as the funeral cortège circum-navigated the large fountain and came to a gradual stop outside the entrance to the graveyard.

Somewhat fortunately, Elliot Carr's family had decided on a full burial as opposed to a cremation, in line with Elliot's personal wishes. Although Warner had his own theories, he was thankful that this would at least keep his options open as well as helping him avoid any potential confrontations which might have occurred should the family have wanted a cremation. In that case, he would have to have been absolutely certain that there was no chance of foul play. Just recently, that theory had become somewhat rockier.

He scurried away towards the road as his mobile phone trilled and warbled in his pocket, pulling it out and answering it. It was Hardwick.

'I presume you're at the funeral?' Hardwick asked.

'Yes, which is precisely why I can't take phone calls right now, Hardwick. So if you don't mind—'

'I just thought you might like to know that we're on our way to Brighton,' Hardwick said, interrupting him.

'That's lovely. Get me a stick of rock, will you?' Warner replied sarcastically. 'What is this, a bloody social call?'

'We're going there to speak to Owen Bartlett. The real Owen Bartlett. You see, he's been giving us the runaround for some reason and there's something not quite right about that.'

Something not quite right about not wanting to spend your day talking to Kempston Hardwick and Ellis Flint? Warner thought. *Surely not.*

'I don't know how many times I need to tell you this, Hardwick, but you can't just go around—'

'If I were you, Detective Inspector, I'd have the burial halted. Or at least make sure there's an officer near the grave at all times until we know what's gone on. You never know what evidence might be on the body.'

'Well you're not me, are you, Hardwick?' Warner barked. 'Our forensics team has taken every scrap of potential evidence, investigated it and stored it. Quite frankly, they're the experts and you're not. You're just a complete pain in the backside, if I'm perfectly honest.'

'Detective Inspector, can I just—'

'No, you cannot. You can stop calling me, stop visiting me and stop interfering. This is my investigation, so keep your nose out of it.' Warner pulled his phone away from his ear and went to press the *call end* button, but not before bringing the phone back to his ear again. 'Oh, and Hardwick? Don't forget my bloody stick of rock.'

He hung up the phone and held down the button to switch it off. Regardless of how important any incoming calls might be, he knew that his focus now had to be on the guests at Elliot Carr's funeral.

48

The atmosphere on the train carriage on the way to Brighton was subdued yet tense, with Hardwick fidgeting and looking generally quite agitated between periods of confusion and quietude.

'I just don't understand it, Ellis. What does Owen Bartlett have to hide? I mean, on the face of it he looks like a suspect because he disappears into thin air on the night a man dies at his place of work. Then we find out he couldn't have been responsible because Elliot Carr died well after Owen had left. But it's possible, isn't it, that he could have been involved. If Elliot Carr had taken longer than expected to die, that is. If it had been particularly slow, there's no reason why he couldn't have done it. But why would he? And anyway, he can't have killed Kimberly Gray or Rosie Blackburn because he was in Brighton at the time. So unless we're looking at two or more killers with the exact same methods, it rules him out again. So why go to the trouble of throwing in a decoy when we came down to speak to him before?'

'I dunno,' Ellis said. 'Maybe it was the decoy's idea. Might not be Owen's fault at all.'

'That's a good point,' Hardwick said. 'What did you say the man you spoke to looked like again?'

'Much lighter hair, cut very short if not shaved. Can't really remember much otherwise,' Ellis said. 'I'd had a bit to drink afterwards.'

'How tall would you say he was? Compared to you, I mean,' Hardwick asked.

'Uh, probably about the same. Why?'

'Because the man I spoke to was about three inches taller.' Hardwick thought back to the time he spent in Owen Bartlett's mother's living room. That was it! The photographs. There were photographs of the man he'd believed to be Owen, his mother and another young man with short, light hair. His brother.

Now that Hardwick had discovered this, Ellis had expected him to leap off the train and march towards Owen Bartlett's house at an even faster pace than usual. On the contrary, he stepped slowly onto the platform and shuffled along the platform, his brow furrowed.

'Something the matter, Kempston?' Ellis asked, a little confused.

'Yes, but I don't know what,' Hardwick replied. 'I mean, why would he do that? If he was more than willing to speak to me himself, with my reputation, then why would he send his brother just to speak to you, Ellis? No offence meant, of course.'

'None taken,' Ellis said, not quite sure he understood where the offence was anyway. 'Unless, of course, it was the other way round. And you spoke to the brother and I spoke to the real Owen?' he suggested.

'Possible, Ellis. Possible. There's only one way to find out, really, isn't there?'

The pair headed to the Evening Star, a small, traditional pub within spitting distance of Brighton station. Ellis, of course, had already been here before but Hardwick was pleasantly surprised at the gentle atmosphere and the impressive range of beers on offer.

'No Campari, I'm afraid,' Ellis said.

'Oh, not to worry, Ellis. I think there's more than enough choice on the beer front for me.'

Ellis ordered a pint of local bitter and Hardwick opted for a glass of Norwegian stout — a light tipple at 10.4% — and the pair sat down at a table by the window.

'Now,' Hardwick said, before taking a sip of his beer. 'According to his Facebook profile, Owen Bartlett has been working at the Strawberry Fields hotel on New Steine.'

'On what?' Ellis asked, settling his pint down on a damp beer mat.

'It's a road, Ellis. Give me your phone.'

Ellis did as he was told.

'Now, look at this,' Hardwick said, pointing to Owen Bartlett's Facebook profile, which he'd pulled up on the screen. 'He posted earlier this morning that he's got a rare day off so was going to sit at home catching up on some DVD box sets. That means he'll be at home right now.'

'Ah, but so might his brother,' Ellis said. 'We can't just go marching round there.'

'I'm not suggesting that, Ellis,' Hardwick replied. 'Do let me finish. What I'm suggesting is that one of us calls Owen Bartlett on the mobile number he has listed on his Facebook profile, withholding our number, and pretends to be someone from the Strawberry Fields hotel, asking him to pop in for half an hour to help with something. We'll say he'll get paid double or something, make it worth his while. We'll wait at the end of his street, between his house and Strawberry Fields. That way we'll find out who the real Owen Bartlett is. He wouldn't be able to send a brother who looks nothing like him into work for him.'

'That's pure genius, Kempston,' Ellis said, before downing his pint in one go. 'Come on, then. Let's go!'

'Not just yet, Ellis,' Hardwick said, settling back into his chair. 'There's no rush.'

'Oh,' Ellis said, blinking rapidly and looking a little disappointed. 'Well, I'll go and get another one then.'

49

Jez Cook had a face like thunder as the door to the interview room opened and Detective Inspector Rob Warner walked in and sat down.

'Jeremy, lovely to meet you again,' Warner said, extending his hand.

'My friends call me Jez,' came the terse reply.

'I know they do, Jeremy. How have you been recently? It's been a little while since we've crossed paths.'

'That's because I've been keeping my nose clean. So I dunno why you dragged me in here. No, scrap that. I don't know why you got your little lapdog to drag me in here,' he said, gesturing towards Detective Constable Sam Kerrigan, who was sat next to Warner, closest to the sound recorder, which wasn't turned on.

'Making sure you don't get caught isn't the same as keeping your nose clean, Jeremy,' Warner said, smiling.

'And no-one dragged you in here. You were asked to voluntarily attend an interview.'

'Voluntarily?' Jez said, snorting. 'Not much bloody voluntary about that, was there?'

'Were you arrested?' Warner asked, casually glancing at his notepad.

'Well, no.'

'Then it was voluntary. You're free to go at any time.' Jez looked at the two detectives and then at the door. 'But then you wouldn't have your next little bit of gossip for your mates on the street, would you? Let me do you a deal, Jeremy. We can do a little bit of an information swap. What do you say?'

'I ain't no grass,' Jez replied, folding his arms.

'I'm not asking you to grass. It's an information swap. You might not even have any information which can help me. And to make it even more attractive, I'm going to give you my information first.'

Jez sat silently for a few moments before speaking. 'What information?'

'About the deaths at the Manor Hotel in South Heath. I know you've shown an interest because you've been asking about it at the Freemason's Arms in Tollinghill.' Warner raised his hand as Jez opened his mouth to speak. 'And I'm not accusing you of anything. It's only natural to show an interest. Now, do you know anything about what happened there?'

'No. I don't. And I'm entitled to a brief so can I have one please?'

'That's only if you're arrested, Jeremy. And you've not been arrested. Should you be arrested?'

Jez said nothing.

'Good. As I said, I'll give you my information first. Call it a gesture of goodwill. Between you and me and these four walls, there's been a third death at the Manor Hotel.' Warner saw Jez's eyes light up. 'Now, all I want you to do is keep your ear to the ground for me. If you hear anything about what's gone on down there, I want you to call me, all right?'

'What, so you think there's a serial killer around? You're actually taking it seriously now?' Jez asked, leaning forward.

Warner leaned forward to mirror his body language. 'I'm saying it's a distinct possibility. But that is *not* public knowledge, nor do I want it to be. Is that clear? If that gets out, I'll know exactly who it's down to and believe me I've got a filing cabinet as tall as you full of unsolved crimes which only need a suspect. Still on a suspended sentence, aren't you?' Jez said nothing, clearly understanding the situation. 'Trust me. If someone around here is killing people for whatever reason — some sick, twisted game or whatever it is, I'm going to make sure they're caught. All I'm asking is that you hug on tightly to that grapevine, all right? And if it starts to rustle, call me straight away.'

Jez swallowed hard and nodded. 'Right you are.'

50

Hardwick and Flint got into position at the end of St George's Terrace, where it met Upper Bedford Street, crouched behind a low wall. They knew Owen would have to walk this way, then west up Upper St James's Street before turning towards the sea front and onto New Steine. Hardwick punched 141 followed by Owen Bartlett's number into Ellis's mobile phone.

'Hello, Owen?' Hardwick said, speaking in a slightly higher-pitched generic foreign accent. 'Is Fabio here from Strawberry Fields. I am new here today and I am having trouble booking some guests in their room. Could you help me please?'

'Uh, is Anna not there?' Owen asked.

'No, she had to pop out,' Hardwick said. 'She said call Owen if I have any problems. She said you know what to do and are very helpful.'

Hardwick heard Owen sighing at the other end of the line.

'Right, okay. I'll come down.'

'How long will you be?' Hardwick asked. 'Is quite urgent.'

'Don't worry, I'm coming now. I'll be five minutes max.'

'Thank you!' Hardwick said, hanging up the phone to see Ellis was glaring at him.

'Bit racist, isn't it?' Ellis said.

'What, doing a foreign accent? Hardly. If you mean the broken English, it was a safeguard just in case he started asking any awkward questions. I could just pretend I didn't understand or was new here.'

Within thirty seconds, Owen Bartlett was jogging down the steps from his front door and walking towards where Hardwick and Flint were crouched. Hardwick could see that it was the Owen he spoke to, with the longer dark hair and not the blonder one who Ellis now knew to be the brother.

As he reached the end of the street, Hardwick stood up and blocked his path.

'Ah, Mr Bartlett. How lovely to see you again. I presume you remember me?' Owen nodded as Hardwick spoke. 'And my colleague here?'

'Uh no, I don't think I do.'

'Oh no! Of course!' Hardwick said. 'Because it wasn't you who spoke to him, was it? It was your brother.'

'Sorry?' Owen said, looking genuinely confused.

'When my colleague Ellis here came down to speak to you before I did, it wasn't you he spoke to. Your brother stopped him at the door and spoke to him instead, pretending to be you.'

'What? Why would he do that?' Owen said.

'I think that's something you'd better tell us, don't you?' Hardwick replied.

A flash of realisation broke across Owen's face.

'Ah, I see you've had an epiphany,' Hardwick said. 'Now, why don't you tell us all about it?'

'I can't, I've got to get to work and help somebody out. Later, maybe, yeah?'

'No, is no problem,' Hardwick said, reverting to the voice he'd used on the phone. 'Fabio has magically fixed the problem.'

Owen looked at Hardwick, let out a half-laugh and shook his head.

The three walked to the Sidewinder pub in almost complete silence, before ordering drinks and sitting down at a sun-drenched wooden table next to the window.

'You know, this is where your brother brought me,' Ellis said to Owen. 'I think you should probably tell us why, too, because this isn't looking too good for you right now.'

Owen's head fell, his chin resting on his chest. 'If I tell you, will you promise to believe me that I had nothing to do with anyone dying? I promise you, it's really difficult for me to explain and I feel dreadful about it, but I didn't do anything.'

'If you say you had nothing to do with it, and if that's true, then what you say will be treated in the strictest confidence,' Hardwick said. 'We just need to find out who killed Elliot Carr, Kimberly Gray and Rosie Blackburn.'

'I can't help with the deaths. I don't know anything about those. All I know is why I left the Manor Hotel so quickly and suddenly and why my brother decided to pretend to be me the other day. And I promise you, I had nothing to do with that. He never even told me about it. He was probably just trying to protect me,'

'Protect you from what?' Ellis said.

'From myself,' Owen replied. 'He knows I'm not good with talking to people and that I get flustered under pressure. He's so much calmer and better with things like this, so I think he was just protecting me to stop me getting into trouble. God, I really don't know how to say this. Look, Elliot Carr wasn't quite the man he made out he was. All right?'

'And how can you say that based on having only spoken to him for a couple of hours?' Hardwick asked.

'Because what sort of man goes away for his wedding anniversary and has a fumble with a male hotel worker while his wife is in their room upstairs?'

Hardwick blinked as he tried to piece everything together. 'You mean...'

'Yes. I'm gay. And so was Elliot Carr but he wouldn't have admitted it. He certainly didn't seem very happily married when he was trying to get into my pants that night at the hotel.'

'Uh, if I may ask, could you tell us a little more?' Hardwick asked. 'About how it all came about. When and where. Not the details, obviously.'

'He was going on about his wife and what she was like, more and more as he drank. I've got a well developed gaydar, you see. It gets pretty well-honed living in Brighton. I know I was stupid, but I started flirting a bit and things got out of hand. I asked him to help me get something from the store room, and... Well, you said you didn't want the details.'

'This store room,' Hardwick asked. 'Would that be room thirteen on the top floor?'

'Yeah, it is. No-one really goes up there much. Only Barbara and sometimes me. People reckon it's haunted but I don't believe in all that so I'm happy enough going up there. Otherwise it's only people we can somehow convince to go.'

'So why did you have to leave so suddenly?' Ellis asked. 'I'm not sure I understand.'

'Because we were caught, weren't we?' Owen said. 'Barbara came in and found us. She dragged me out and told me I had to go. She gets a bit funny like that. I mean, I know it was unprofessional of me and that I'd be sacked from any job for doing that, but she gave different reasons. Like saying it was unnatural and wicked, and all that.'

'She said that?' Ellis asked. 'Has she made comments like that before?'

'Well, not openly. I think she made some remark about it when I first started working there. When I said I came from Brighton she made some comment about had I moved up here to "get away from the queers" or something. She said it like a joke, and I thought maybe it was just tongue in cheek humour. I was new there so didn't want to say anything and to be honest I forgot all about it until the incident in the store room, when things started to make a bit more sense.'

'So when she asked you to leave, what did you do?'

'I left, obviously. I would've been sacked by the big bosses anyway and I was just ashamed at what I'd done. Not like that, I mean. Ashamed that I'd been unprofessional and let my guard down. I really didn't want to hang around there any longer and wait for Barbara to start telling everyone. She's a gossip at the best of times.'

'If it helps,' Ellis said, 'as far as we know she didn't tell anyone. We spoke to a few of your colleagues about you leaving and none of this was ever mentioned.'

'Oh. Well maybe she has got a conscience after all,' Owen said, stopping to take a long drag of his drink. His voice seemed to be getting croakier as he spoke. A sign of stress, Hardwick presumed. 'But that's why I had to go. I wasn't going to hang around a minute longer. I felt embarrassed and abused.'

'I can understand that,' Hardwick said. 'So was that the last time you saw Elliot Carr?'

'Yes. I went straight downstairs, grabbed my bag and

my coat and went. He was still upstairs in room thirteen when I left.'

'This was just before eleven o'clock, was it?' Hardwick asked. Owen nodded in response. 'And at that time, Elliot Carr was left all alone in room thirteen, where he was to die about half an hour later, in the company of one person. Barbara Hills.'

51

The ringing of DI Warner's office phone told him it was internal call. He picked up the receiver and barked his name.

'DI Warner, Kit Daniels is at front desk to see you. He says it's urgent.'

Warner sighed heavily. 'Great. I'll come down and get him.'

When Warner got to the front desk, Kit Daniels stood up and put out his hand to shake it. After a second, Warner shook his hand quickly and limply.

'If you're not here to apologise and give me a written guarantee that you're dropping your daft story on the Manor Hotel, I'm not interested,' he said.

'I don't think there's any danger of me saying or doing that, DI Warner. In fact, I've got a bone to pick with you.'

Warner let out a hearty laugh. 'Have you now? And who do you think you are exactly?'

'I'm the reporter who's just found out that you've been lying to me and keeping public interest information from the public. Two words: Rosie Blackburn.'

Warner blew air through his nostrils and beckoned Kit Daniels towards the lift. 'We'll talk in my office.'

When they'd reached the third floor and Warner had closed his office door behind him, he sat down behind his desk, crossed his arms and looked pointedly at Kit Daniels.

'Go on then. Tell me what you think you know.'

'I *know* that Rosie Blackburn died in room thirteen at the Manor Hotel and that she died in the same way as Elliot Carr and Kimberly Gray. And I know that you're treating this differently now because you attended the scene yourself. Would it be fair to say that you think the deaths might be linked somehow?' Kit said with a smirk on his face.

'Who told you all this?' was all that Warner could bring himself to say.

'All journalists have sources, DI Warner. If I revealed mine, they wouldn't bother giving me any more information, would they?'

Warner gritted his teeth and tried to steady his breathing. 'If you've got someone feeding you police information or information on a crime which isn't public knowledge, you're committing a crime.'

Kit Daniels smirked confidently. 'Oh, come on. You know damn well that we haven't published anything that you hadn't intended to release as information. We just happen to get there a bit quicker than you do. Perhaps you should see that more as an indicator of problems that need fixing at your end rather than ours.'

'I haven't even seen you at the scene of the incidents yet. What's different this time, Kit?' Warner asked, folding his arms. 'As I see it, you're either sneaking in afterwards and speaking to witnesses on the sly or even worse, you've got a source on my side of the fence. And before you say it, that's not a possibility I'm willing to entertain.'

'You weren't willing to entertain the possibility of anything linking the deaths of Elliot Carr and Kimberly Gray, were you? And you've already backtracked pretty quickly on that.'

'Are you making accusations against my officers?' Warner asked, trying to look as stern as he possibly could. He knew even this wouldn't warn Kit Daniels off, but it was worth the try.

'I never said anything of the sort. As for your "witnesses",' Kit said, using his hands to indicate inverted commas, 'Is there anything to say that I can't ask my own questions of innocent members of the public as well?'

'There is if you're trying to ask them leading questions to get one of your sensationalist headlines again. And you're assuming that they *are* all innocent members of the public.'

'Ah-ha. And there we have it,' Kit said, cocking his head and pointing at DI Warner. 'Would it be fair to say, then, that you consider one or more of your witnesses to actually be suspects?'

Warner sat silently for a couple of moments before speaking slowly and quietly.

'I think it's time you left, Kit.'

52

Barely thirty seconds after Kit Daniels left Warner's office, the phone rang. The display showed him it was an internal call from forensics.

'Yes?' he said as he picked up the phone, with a voice that sounded tired and resigned.

'Sounds like you're having a good day, then, Rob,' the voice of Mark Ayres said.

'No worse than usual,' Warner replied. 'What have you got for me?'

'It's just a little something I thought you might be interested in. It wasn't even noticed at first, but we've got a new starter with us at the moment who's a little... Shall we say keen? Anyway, she spotted something in the photos. She's one of those studiers, who's always so happy to relay whatever she's read in the latest forensics book. Pain in the backside most of the time, but in this case it's been pretty handy—'

'Look, can you just get to the point please?' Warner asked, not much fancying another half an hour on the phone while Mark Ayres dithered and dallied before finally saying what he had to say.

'Sure. Long story short, the knots used for the nooses were what interested her. Elliot Carr and Rosie Blackburn's were both tied by someone right-handed. We called the families of Elliot Carr, Kimberly Gray and Rosie Blackburn. Elliot and Rosie were both right-handed, but Kimberly was left-handed. The knot which was used on her noose was tied by someone left-handed.'

'What, so they tied their own knots?'

'So it seems. Either that or by some sheer coincidence they were killed by different people — people who had the same dominant hand as they did. I'm no mathematician, but that seems unlikely to me. From what I've read, around 13% of men and 11% of women are left-handed. Doesn't seem all that likely that they had different killers not only using the same method but having the same dominant hand as them. No, I'd say they almost certainly tied their own nooses.'

'What about DNA and fibres? Anything else on the nooses?'

'Plenty. But you'd expect that, considering how many guests and people stay at the hotel and come into contact with these things. You'd have an ice cube's chance in hell of finding anything conclusive on that basis.'

Warner felt both vindicated and utterly confused. If

they all killed themselves, why? They were all unconnected to each other and seemingly not in a frame of mind
to want to end their own lives, yet the evidence showed
that they almost certainly did.

FRIDAY 27TH MARCH

53

It seemed to Hardwick that every stone he uncovered just led him down another alleyway with no conclusion. The whole case had seemed far simpler at the start with just one body and a simple case of a couple of suspects and the additional possibility of it being a suicide. It was usually the case with these sorts of things that more deaths made it easier to catch the killer, as patterns could be spotted and potential suspects eliminated through alibis and the like. In this case, though, it just made things more confusing.

Every death had brought with it new possibilities, sometimes new suspects and undoubtedly far more confusion for both Hardwick and Flint. At times like this, Hardwick knew it was prudent to return to the start and centre himself in the moment. With that in mind, they'd returned to the Manor Hotel to enjoy one of their famous afternoon teas.

Hardwick closed his eyes as he sat back in the large

armchair and chomped on a scone, the dough sticking to the roof of his mouth as the clotted cream teased his tastebuds.

Ellis, on the other hand, sipped at his cup of tea then added an extra spoonful of sugar. He was trying to keep himself calm and his stress levels — positive or negative — down. Since his meeting with Dr Harding, he'd been worrying more and more about what he'd read online was known as the "silent killer" of stress. Of course, worrying about stress was rather a self-fulfilling prophecy, so he'd moved on to reading up about meditation and relaxation. Ellis had never been the most stressed out person in the world, particularly not compared with Hardwick. Still, there would be no harm in him trying to relax a little more.

'Hello, my loves,' came the familiar voice from behind Hardwick as Barbara sidled up alongside their table. 'Everything all right?'

'Yes, thank you,' Ellis said. 'Lovely tea. How are things here?'

'Oh, fine, fine. Are you here on business or pleasure?'

'Bit of both,' Ellis replied, sensing that Hardwick was focused more on piecing something together in his head than he was on engaging in conversation.

'Well, if there's anything I can help you with, just give me a shout. I've got to pop out for half an hour, though. Mandy will be looking after the bar if you want anything,' Barbara said.

Ellis smiled and nodded before taking another sip of

his tea. He swirled the hot liquid around his mouth as his eyebrows narrowed.

'Kempston, I'm just thinking...'

Hardwick didn't even open his eyes to speak. 'Ellis, if this is another one of your—'

'No, no. Listen to me. That Mandy's always on the front desk, isn't she? She's like a permanent fissure or whatever it's called. She'd see everyone who came in and out of the hotel.'

'Yes and she's already said no-one of any note came in or out around the time the three people died, apart from Owen Bartlett.'

'Still something not right about him,' Ellis said. 'Fancy sitting at the bar?'

'I'm quite comfortable here, thank you, Ellis,' Hardwick replied, his eyes still closed and his head back.

'Oh, all right then. I'm going to go up and speak to this Mandy. See what she remembers.'

'On second thoughts, Ellis,' Hardwick said, shooting up from his seat, 'I might just come with you. Just to... Well, just to make sure.'

'To make sure I don't say anything stupid?' Ellis asked. Hardwick said nothing.

Mandy smiled as the two sat down at the bar, Ellis with his pot of tea and Hardwick with one final untouched buttered scone on his side plate.

'Hello, back again?' she said cheerily.

'Yep, can't get enough of this tea,' Ellis said. 'Who's

looking after reception if you're in here? I was under the impression that was your area.'

'Oh, it is. But it's not exactly busy around here at the moment, as you know. The reception isn't exactly the neediest part of the hotel right now. Anyway, there's a bell that rings through to here if anyone should turn up. Which I doubt.'

'All this stuff been bad for business?' Ellis asked, knowing perfectly well that it'd been disastrous.

'Yeah, other than a few weird ghost hunter types or the sickos who like to turn up to places where people have died. Not the sort of people the Belvedere group want in here, to be honest, so they'd rather we turn them away than take their money.'

'Ah. And how are the staff taking it?'

'The only way we can take it, really. Hope that things pick up soon. I think a couple of people are looking at other jobs, just in case. Barbara mentioned retirement. To be honest, she should probably have retired years ago. She did, I think, but started working here as she couldn't bear sitting at home on her own.'

'She must enjoy her work, then,' Ellis said.

'Well, yes. I think she enjoys her position more, between you and me. I think having had a fairly important job in the past when she was a lawyer, she likes to put herself in a position of importance here. That's one of the reasons I try to stay on reception. To be honest, she scares me.'

'Scares you?' Ellis said, noticing that Hardwick's eyebrows had risen.

'Yeah. Don't tell her I said that, though. I wouldn't dare say it while she was in the building, either, as she's got supersonic hearing. The whole place is run by corporate area managers who we never see, but as far as us bottom-rung staff are concerned, she's pretty much put herself in charge. She knows everything that goes on, has her own little ways and rituals. The other day she told me off for "taking the Lord's name in vain". I only said "Jesus Christ" because she mentioned that every booking that night had cancelled.'

'That's a bit odd,' Ellis said, looking at Hardwick.

'Yes, it is,' Hardwick replied. 'She didn't strike me as being particularly religious.'

'She made some comment about Mandy using bad language when we were here the other day after Rosie Blackburn was found,' Ellis added. 'She'd only said "Jesus Christ" then, too.'

'Has she done anything like that before?' Hardwick asked Mandy.

'A couple of times, yeah. And I didn't think she was but a couple of months ago she started wearing a necklace with a crucifix on it and became a bit more... Well, uppity is the word, I suppose. I didn't think much of it. Just the way some people get when they get old, I suppose.'

'Barbara Hills lives in, doesn't she?' Hardwick asked.

'Yeah, she does. She never got married or had kids, so she rents her house out and lives in here at the hotel. She's basically always working, which probably explains why she gets a bit uptight sometimes.'

Hardwick thought for a moment or two, working out his angle of attack.

'Maybe she experienced something odd, too,' Hardwick suggested. 'Perhaps she's seen the ghost that haunts the place.'

Ellis looked at Hardwick with confusion. Had he finally come around to the idea of some sort of paranormal involvement?

'I dunno, possibly,' Mandy said. 'Her room's nowhere near where the other stuff is supposed to have happened, though.'

'Oh? That's odd, then. Where's her room?' Hardwick asked.

'At the back of the hotel, far end of the corridor if you turn right at the top of the stairs on the first floor. Nowhere near room thirteen.'

'Ah, yes, you're right. Seems unlikely, then,' Hardwick said, glancing at his watch. 'Blimey, is that the time? We're meant to be in Tollinghill in ten minutes. We'd better get going. Come along, Ellis,' he said, ushering Ellis off his chair and out of the bar before he could protest. 'Thank you for your time, Mandy.'

'No problem. Let me know if I can help any more,' said the quietening voice as Hardwick and Flint scurried out towards reception.

'What's going on, Kempston? We don't have to be—'

Hardwick raised his hand to indicate that Ellis should

stop speaking. 'Ellis, I want you to do me a favour. I want you to stand outside the front door. If Barbara Hills returns, keep her busy. Whatever you do, don't let her go upstairs.'

'Why?' Ellis asked, now utterly confused. 'Where are you going?'

'I'm going to do something I should have done a long time ago, Ellis,' Hardwick replied, before turning and walking up the stairs.

54

Fortunately for Hardwick, the fact that the Manor Hotel tried to remain as traditional as possible meant that there were no fancy electronic card-swipe entry systems to the rooms, but a nice standard pin tumbler lock. Hardwick fumbled around in his inside jacket pocket and removed a bump key. Having already seen the type of locks on the staff doors from his last visit here with DI Warner, he'd made sure he'd come prepared this time.

He slotted the bump key fully into the lock and then pulled it out gently until he heard one single click. He turned the key anti-clockwise and at the same time struck the end of the key with his heavy metal fountain pen, wincing visibly as he did so. The key turned and the door clicked open.

Hardwick ensured that the door could be opened from the inside without a key, then he removed the bump key and closed the door quietly behind him.

Barbara's room was made to look more like a home bedroom than a hotel room. It was decorated with a number of personal nicknacks, but it was the large crucifix on the wall above the headboard that grasped his attention. He walked over to the window and looked out through the net curtain, getting his bearings and realising that he didn't have a view of the road or the driveway and wouldn't know when Barbara was coming back. Although he had instructed Ellis to keep a look out and stop her from coming up, Ellis was hardly the most reliable of watchmen. Hardwick knew he'd have to act quickly.

He began to open cupboards and drawers, quickly rifling through for anything of note which might help him out. At the back of the wardrobe, under a pile of warm winter jumpers, Hardwick noticed what felt like a photograph album.

He pulled it out, set it on the bed and opened the album. It didn't contain photos, but instead a number of press cuttings going back some forty years. They all appeared to be in chronological order, relating to criminal trials. He scan-read a couple and realised they were all cases in which Barbara had acted as either the defending or prosecuting solicitor. There didn't seem to be any theme, and Hardwick supposed that this must be a complete record of all of the trials in which she was involved, catalogued in some sort of memory book. Not quite the murderer's narcissistic catalogue of destruction that you'd find in a cheap detective novel, he thought. On the contrary, this album detailed quite a few of her unsuccessful times in court.

It was then that Hardwick heard the key being put into the lock and the door handle being turned.

55

Ellis was sick of this. He was always relegated to keeping an eye out or running daft errands for Hardwick and never got to get involved with any of the juicy parts of detection. Even when he did, Hardwick wasn't happy. This was despite the fact that more often than not it was Ellis, not Hardwick, who managed to solve the crimes or at least provide the clue which led to them being solved, albeit usually completely inadvertently.

He shoved his hands in his jacket pockets as he paced backwards and forwards on the gravel outside the front door, grumbling to himself as he did so. He couldn't even hear a car or person, never mind see one, and with the long sweeping gravel driveway laid out in front of him he knew he'd certainly hear something coming before he saw it.

The fact of the matter was that the place was deserted. There would be no cars trundling up the driveway, happy holidaymakers dragging their suitcases from the boot, beaming as they admired the beautiful architecture of the Manor Hotel, delighted that the reality matched or exceeded their expectations or the pictures they'd seen on the internet. Not today. Not now, after all that had gone on recently. All he could hear was the distant barking of a dog and his own heavy sighs as he got progressively more annoyed at Kempston the more he dwelled on it.

Finally, he stopped pacing and leaned back against one of the stone pillars outside the entranceway to the hotel. He knew he'd just have to suck it up and accept it for now, but he'd certainly be having words with Kempston later. Either this was an equal partnership or it wasn't. He grumbled again, then pulled his mobile phone out of his trouser pocket. He swiped across the screen, entered his pin number and tapped to open the *Alien Annihilation* 2 game. It would be one way of releasing his frustrations.

56

Hardwick took a deep breath as the door creaked open and Barbara Hills walked into the room. From his hiding spot in the recess between the wardrobe and the far wall, he knew he couldn't be seen. Yet.

The voice came unexpectedly and suddenly. 'I know you're in here, so why don't you come out and tell me why?'

Hardwick jammed his eyes shut and tried to pretend he hadn't heard it, but he knew it was futile. He stepped forward and tried desperately to think of an excuse to give Barbara as to why he was hiding in her private room.

'Uh... Room service?' he said.

'Very funny,' Barbara replied, a deadly serious look on her face. 'But why don't we start being honest and truthful with each other? After all, I'm sure you want me to be honest and truthful with you.'

'Do you want to be honest and truthful with me?' Hardwick asked, stalling for time and trying to gauge Barbara's mood and thought process.

'It makes no difference to me,' she said. 'Not now. But why don't I try and guess why you're here? You're here because you don't think those three people did commit suicide, do you? You think they were killed. And you don't know who by, but you have an inkling that I'm involved somewhere along the line so you came up here to search my room, knowing I was out. Sorry, *thinking* I was out.'

'You told us you were going out,' Hardwick said.

'I did, yes. And it's a good job I did, isn't it? Else we wouldn't be here having this conversation now.'

'What's this all about, Barbara?' Hardwick asked, trying to sound more like a caring friend than a suspicious private detective.

'You're expecting me to act the innocent, aren't you?' she replied, sitting on the bed. 'You're expecting me to be shocked and upset when you accuse me of having something to do with their deaths. The fact is that it really doesn't matter.' Barbara lowered her head.

'What do you mean?' Hardwick asked.

'I mean it really doesn't matter. Sooner or later, the outcome will be the same. And right now I think I'd rather avoid the ignominy and ensure it's sooner.' As she spoke, Barbara ran her hand underneath the mattress, feeling for something.

'Are you looking for this?' Hardwick said, pulling a small revolver from his inside jacket pocket. Barbara stared emotionlessly at him, not moving. 'There is no easy escape, Barbara. Now why don't you tell me what this is all about? Why do you keep a gun under your bed?'

'Do it,' Barbara said, without an ounce of emotion in her voice. 'Pull the trigger. Save me the job.'

'No. I want you to tell me what's going on,' Hardwick replied.

Barbara laughed. 'Are you stupid? I can head for that door right now and there will be two possible outcomes. Either you'll shoot me and kill me or I'll walk out and die anyway. I'm ill. Very ill. Ovarian cancer. Stage four. Nothing you can do now will make any difference at all. I've made my peace.'

'Is that what you call it?' Hardwick asked. 'Making your peace? What's peaceful about killing people?'

Barbara's eyes visibly darkened. 'Do you know what it's like to spend your life defending people who can't be defended? To know that through a technicality of law you're responsible for society's vilest villains walking free? For murderers, rapists and child molesters to be able to offend again? When I found out I was dying, God found me. I knew that He was punishing me for what I'd done and I knew I needed to make amends.'

Hardwick had come face to face with ruthless killers a number of times in his life and knew that keeping calm and rational was his only hope of not becoming the next victim. 'How did killing those three people make amends for what you did as a lawyer, Barbara?'

'The Lord knows who he wants in the Kingdom of

Heaven,' Barbara replied, making the sign of the cross as she looked up at the crucifix hanging over her bed. 'Even someone like you must be familiar with the Ten Commandments. Number seven: Thou shalt not commit adultery. Not to mention Leviticus 20:13. If there is a man who lies with a male as those who lie with a woman, both of them have committed a detestable act; they shall surely be put to death. Their bloodguiltness is upon them.'

Hardwick stiffened as he realised the extent of Barbara's Christian fundamentalism. He had always been greatly worried by the way so many people lived their lives based around what was written in a book a couple of thousand years ago. Faith was one thing, but when it affected other people's lives it was a whole different matter. 'Elliot Carr?' he asked.

Barbara nodded. 'I found them.'

'Owen said. But why only kill Elliot?' Hardwick asked.

'Two would've been daft. Owen was embarrassed and mortified. I told him that unless he wanted to be outed and have his name tainted, he should go back to that pit of hell with the rest of them.'

'Brighton?' Hardwick asked, having heard the town called many things in the past, but a pit of hell was a new one on him.

Barbara nodded again. 'Do you know the first two commandments? "You shall have no other gods before Me" and "You shall not make false idols".'

Hardwick realised his mouth had fallen open. 'You

killed an eighteen-year-old woman because she idolised a pop star?'

'You shall not make false idols!' Barbara screamed. 'You shall have no other gods before Me! And you know exactly why the other one had to die. I know you do.'

The sick feeling welled up in the pit of Hardwick's stomach. *Thou shalt not kill.* 'That was not Rosie Blackburn's choice, and you know it. There were complications with the birth. It happens.'

'The Lord God says otherwise,' Barbara said, again making the sign of the cross.

'Thou shalt not kill?' Hardwick asked. 'That child died through no fault of her own. You've killed three people. How will the Lord judge you?'

'He has already judged me. What do you think this illness is? That is my judgement. I will die early. The least I can hope for now is to spare the flames of Hell and to find peace.'

'How did you do it?' Hardwick asked in a low voice, as calmly as he could muster.

'Oh, I didn't. They did it all themselves. I gave them all a choice. They could either stand on the chair, tie their noose and feel what it was like to face their final judgement or they could take the quick exit courtesy of my little friend there,' she replied, pointing to the gun.

'You held a gun to their heads and made them tie a noose around their own necks?'

'They had a choice. They all chose to repent.'

'They probably thought that way they had a chance of getting out alive. But they never did, did they? Whichever way you look at it, you killed three people,' Hardwick reiterated.

'Three heathens. Three people who sinned in the eyes of the Lord. Do you know how many sinners I let walk free? That is why God punished me. That is why no more sinners must walk free. My body is already punished, but I can save my soul.'

Hardwick took two deep breaths. Barbara said nothing, but continued to stare at him.

'What now?' Hardwick asked.

'Now you'll give me the gun,' Barbara replied.

'What, so you can kill me too? What sins have I committed?'

'I have no desire to kill you. But you can't kill me either. My work is not done.'

Hardwick's eyebrows narrowed. 'Are you saying you want me to let you go on killing more innocent people just so you can feel better about your previous job?'

'They are not innocent people!' Barbara shouted as she began to back towards the door. 'This is for the greater good. Sacrifices must be made for a greater justice to be achieved. You know exactly what I'm talking about. That's why you won't shoot me. That's why you won't chase me. Because I know, Hardwick. I know why you do this. We aren't so different, you and me. Are we?'

Before Hardwick could speak or even decide what to say, the door flew open and thundered into Barbara, sending her sprawling across the floor, banging her head on the skirting board. As she lay unconscious on the carpet, Hardwick looked up to see Ellis Flint standing in the doorway.

'I heard shouting,' Ellis said.

57

Ellis followed Hardwick down the stairs as Barbara was taken away in an ambulance, with Detective Inspector Rob Warner casting his eye over what was going on.

'I listened at the door, Kempston,' Ellis said. 'After she screamed the first time. I heard what she said. Well, some of it anyway.'

'Yes, well, she's a deluded old woman and she needs help. Hopefully now she'll get it.'

'How did she do it?' Ellis asked.

'The gun. If she pointed that thing at you, you'd do what she said, wouldn't you? I should imagine none of them thought she was actually going to kill them. She probably gave them the old Bible spiel while they were stood on the chair with the noose around their necks and they saw it as some kind of punishment or humiliation. You'd sure as hell take your chances, seeing as the alternative was a gunshot and certain death anyway.'

'So did she kick the chair away for them or did she make them kill themselves somehow?'

'We won't know until she's able to speak again, Ellis. We might never know. And does it matter?'

'I suppose not,' Ellis replied as they reached the foot of the stairs and walked into the reception area. 'I need to ask, though. That stuff she said just before I burst in. About knowing why you do this and you two being similar. What was all that about?'

Hardwick swallowed firmly. Before he could speak, DI Rob Warner rounded the corner and slapped his hand down on Hardwick's shoulder.

'Good work, Hardwick. You won't hear me say that often, so stick it in your little memory bank. Although I must say it's not the way I would've gone about it. And I'm going to have an interesting time trying to convince the Super that there's a good reason for your prints being all over the gun. Why didn't you just come to me and tell me that you knew who'd done it?'

'Because I didn't know,' Hardwick replied. 'Not for certain, anyway. It was obvious something wasn't right about Barbara and I took the opportunity to find out for myself.'

'So you broke into her room based on the fact that she seemed a bit weird? Blimey, remind me to upgrade my burglar alarm,' Warner said.

'Good job I did, though, isn't it?'

Warner said nothing, but eventually nodded. 'Well,

let's just keep things a little more... conventional in future, shall we?'

Hardwick chuckled a little. Conventional just wasn't his style.

SATURDAY 28TH MARCH

58

Hardwick ascended the three steps to the sliding door which welcomed him to Shafford General Hospital. Meandering around the queue of people waiting to get to the reception desk, he clocked the blue and white signs pointing visitors in a variety of directions for a multitude of different departments and headed towards the lifts.

It had certainly been a turbulent time recently and the only thing on his mind was rest. The last place he wanted to be right now was in a hospital, one of his least favourite places on the planet.

He made his way down the fourth-floor corridor towards the Joyce Ward and skirted around the reception desk to read the names of the patients on the whiteboard on the wall next to it. He still hadn't found Barbara Hills's name when he was interrupted by the nurse on reception.

'Excuse me, sir. Can I help you?'

'Ah yes, I'm looking for Barbara Hills. I've come to visit,' Hardwick replied.

'I'm afraid we've been told that Mrs Hills is allowed visits from family only,' the nurse said bluntly.

'Yes, I know,' Hardwick said, smiling as pleasantly as he could.

'I was hoping you might swing by,' came the voice of Detective Sergeant Sam Kerrigan. 'Don't worry, love,' he said to the nurse. 'He's with us. Unfortunately.'

The nurse smiled and nodded and went back to her paperwork.

'Very courteous of you, Detective Sergeant,' Hardwick said.

'I thought you might pop in to see how she was getting on,' Kerrigan said as he guided Hardwick towards the private side room Barbara Hills had been put in. 'Fact is, Warner's just left me here to look after her on my own. She's meant to have a police guard at all times, see. All right for him to say that, ain't it? Never bloody him doing these jobs. I haven't eaten for about four hours and me legs are killing me. And, I mean, you're pretty much one of us, ain't you?' Kerrigan said, offering an uncharacteristic amount of plaudits in Hardwick's direction. 'Would you mind watching her just for a few moments while I stretch me legs and grab a bite to eat?'

'Not at all,' Hardwick said, unable to take his eyes off the frail woman lying in the bed in front of him.

'Nice one, cheers,' Kerrigan said. 'Back in five.'

Hardwick slowly approached the bed and sat down on

the chair beside it. He had half expected her to be laid out with tubes sticking out of every orifice, but other than looking particularly weak and world-weary, Barbara appeared to be stable. She was breathing on her own and had only a saline drip connected to her.

'You've finally come to terms with it, haven't you?' Hardwick said quietly. 'I can see it in you. I could see it in your eyes when we were stood in your room. That final acceptance that what's done is done. That you'd done what you needed to do. I meet a lot of people who do a lot of bad things. A lot of people consumed with evil. I may not be the most sociable of people, but I'm a very good judge of character and I know that you don't have an evil bone in your body. What you did, you did for the best of reasons. In your mind. But your personal redemption came at the expense of other people's lives. I know you understand that, and I know you consider their lives to have been expendable. Because of things they did or who they were. But none of them were bad people.

'You know, deep down I'm not so sure there is such a thing as a bad person. People do bad things, but that doesn't make them bad people. They do what they feel is right and just in the circumstances. Just like you did. I understand that. I want you to know that.'

A few minutes later, Hardwick walked back down the steps outside the sliding doors to Shafford General Hospital and opened the door to the phone box a few yards up the road. He dialled Ellis's number, waited for an answer and inserted his change.

'Ellis? It's Hardwick. I'm at Shafford General. I've just been to see Barbara Hills. I'm afraid she passed away in her sleep a few minutes ago. Hmmm? No, no, I don't think so. In fact, she actually seemed rather at peace.'

GET MORE OF MY BOOKS FREE!

Thank you for reading *The Thirteenth Room*. I hope it was as much fun for you as it was for me writing it.

To say thank you, I'd like to invite you to my exclusive *VIP Club*, and give you some of my books and short stories for FREE. All members of my VIP Club have access to FREE, exclusive books and short stories which aren't available anywhere else.

You'll also get access to all of my new releases at a bargain-basement price before they're available anywhere else. Joining is absolutely FREE and you can leave at any time, no questions asked. To join the club, head to adamcroft.net/vip-club **and two free books will be sent to you straight away!**

If you enjoyed the book, please do leave a review on

the site you bought it from. Reviews mean an awful lot to writers and they help us to find new readers more than almost anything else. It would be very much appreciated.

I love hearing from my readers, too, so please do feel free to get in touch with me. You can contact me via my website, on Twitter @adamcroft and you can 'like' my Facebook page at facebook.com/adamcroftbooks.

For more information, visit my website: adamcroft.net

THE WRONG MAN

Kempston Hardwick returns in

THE WRONG MAN

Book launches are rarely exciting. The odd murder tends to spice things up a bit, though.

When famous novelist Rupert Pearson's PA doesn't turn up for his book launch at the Freemason's Arms, he's more annoyed than upset. He certainly didn't expect someone to find her face-down in a ditch.

For Kempston Hardwick, dead PAs are business as usual. Unfortunately. At least there are lots of excuses to visit the pub.

But why had she made so many enemies? Why are the police so keen to fit up an innocent man? And where did Doug's pickled onions go?

Visit adamcroft.net/book/the-wrong-man/ to grab your copy.

ACKNOWLEDGMENTS

My unwavering thanks go to the following people, without whom *The Thirteenth Room* would not have been possible:

Helen Armitage for the extensive information on pathology proceedings and the inner workings of the coroner's court.

Simon Clarke for his number crunching and statistical analysis of suicide rates, murder rates and combining these with statistics on handedness.

David Parry, former Detective Sergeant with Leicestershire Police for his insight and information on police procedures surrounding suspected suicides.

Kate Jones and Charlotte Knowles of the Down's Syndrome Association for spending the time with me to explain more about antenatal screening processes and helping ensure accuracy.

Joanne, Manuela and Jonathan, my editors and beta readers who make sure the book is actually readable.

David Lovesy for the superb cover design.

My wife for her unwavering patience in fixing my plot holes and generally putting the icing on the very rough and unbaked cakes which are my initial drafts and ideas.

Everyone who has asked when my next book will be out and emailed or otherwise contacted me to say how much they love the series. It's your support and love for the books which spurs me on to write more (and faster).

And finally, Mother Nature for ensuring the weather has been too unpleasant for me to want to sit in a pub garden and instead keeping me at my laptop over the winter.

Lightning Source UK Ltd.
Milton Keynes UK
UKHW040953170223
417088UK00004B/140